POEM POEM POEM A POEM FOR EVERY SPRING DAY

First published in the UK 2021 by Macmillan Children's Books, an imprint of Pan Macmillan

This paperback edition published 2026 by Macmillan Children's Books,
an imprint of Pan Macmillan
The Smithson, 6 Briset Street, London EC1M 5NR
EU representative: Macmillan Publishers Ireland Ltd, 1st Floor,
The Liffey Trust Centre, 117–126 Sheriff Street Upper, Dublin 1 D01 YC43
Associated companies throughout the world

ISBN 978-1-0350-4471-9

1 3 5 7 9 8 6 4 2

A CIP catalogue record for this book is available from the British Library.

Printed and bound in the UK using 100% Renewable Electricity by CPI Group (UK) Ltd

MIX
Paper | Supporting responsible forestry
FSC® C116313

POEM POEM POEM POEM A POEM FOR EVERY SPRING DAY

CHOSEN BY ALLIE ESIRI

MACMILLAN

for Eliza Esiri

Also edited by Allie Esiri
from Macmillan

A Poem for Every Summer Day
A Poem for Every Autumn Day
A Poem for Every Winter Day

A Poem for Every Day of the Year

A Poem for Every Night of the Year

Shakespeare for Every Day of the Year

A Poet for Every Day of the Year

A Nursery Rhyme for Every Day of the Year

A Poem for Every Day of Christmas

Contents

April

May

Introduction

In this anthology, the third in a four-part cycle of seasons, you will discover some of the most lively and life-affirming poems ever to be written about spring, and many significant cultural events and historical anniversaries that lie in our calendars between 1 March and 31 May.

There is perhaps no season that has inspired as many poets to pick up their pens (or quills) as spring. In fact, it's almost impossible to name a writer who hasn't responded to these months of verdant renewal and new beginnings. For Gerard Manley Hopkins, who said 'Nothing is so beautiful as Spring', and Christina Rossetti, who wrote 'There is no time like Spring / When life's alive in everything', the season is incomparable in its vitality and splendour. And who could disagree? Not even the infamously curmudgeonly Philip Larkin, better associated with cynicism and gloom, could resist the allure of spring. I can't walk past a blossoming tree in March without thinking of his poem 'The Trees' and its inviting opening lines: 'The trees are coming into leaf / Like something almost being said.'

Given the sheer number of springtime poems that have been composed over the centuries, it's just as well that this anthology offers you not just one, but two pieces of verse for each spring day, almost all of which have been drawn from my anthologies: *A Poem for Every Day of the Year* and *A Poem for Every Night of the Year*. The hope is that the first daily instalment imbues you with the same vivacity and energy that define a dewy spring morning, while the second poem offers an opportunity for gentle reflection and contemplation, and perhaps some ideas to mull over on a balmy night.

As you might expect, there are entries like Wordsworth's 'To My Sister', which extols the joys and sweetness of the season. Of course you'll also find his most anthologized poem, 'I Wandered Lonely as a Cloud', which not only captures the essence of vernal beauty, but encourages us to wander with our minds; to draw on our memories of golden flowers and the enveloping breeze in those moments when we can't experience them directly. But this collection isn't just packed full of romantic, cheerful and bucolic images of nature in bloom and birthing animals. After all, for T. S. Eliot, 'April is the cruellest month'. It certainly does tend to be rainy . . .

What is more, although spring is usually synonymous with new life, growth and vigour, it is for some writers redolent of loss and death. For instance, poets such as A. E. Housman, Linton Kwesi Johnson and the 2020 Nobel Laureate Louise Glück write poignantly of how spring represents a past youth, accessible now only through nostalgic reminiscence.

Some works are even more explicitly tragic and sobering. In his 1915 work 'But These Things Also', the war poet Edward Thomas reminds us that though spring offers hope, it is still inexorably shrouded by traumas past (in this case, the brutal 1914 campaigns of the First World War): 'Spring's here, Winter's not gone.' And over a hundred years later, the spoken word poet Duranka Perera composed a pain-stricken response to the terrorist attacks that wreaked devastation on Easter Sunday 2019, in his native country of Sri Lanka.

Perera's poem is one of several pieces in this collection that relate to specific landmark dates in the calendar rather than the season of spring. International Women's Day on 8 March is celebrated with Maya Angelou's anthem 'Phenomenal

Woman'; Mothering Sunday is recognized with poignant pieces by Stevie Smith and George Hare Leonard, while World Wildlife Day brings us a thought-provoking rebuke of humans' mistreatment of animals by the poet-farmer Wendell Berry. And who better than Lewis Carroll to exhibit the joy of nonsense on April Fool's Day?

World-changing historical moments and events are also made immediate through the brilliance of verse. So, an extract from Shakespeare's *Julius Caesar* transports us to the Roman Senate on the Ides (15) of March as the eponymous general is warned about his imminent assassination; Henry Wadsworth Longfellow lets us ride alongside Paul Revere to deliver his message about the invading British on 18 April 1775, the eve of the American Revolutionary War; and Robert Browning takes us into the French camp where Emperor Napoleon chats to an injured young soldier on 23 April at the 1809 Battle of Ratisbon. Elsewhere, Carol Ann Duffy asks us to imagine what *really* inspired Charles Darwin to write *The Origin of Species* on a day out with his wife on 7 April 1852.

The best poems are those that are able to immerse us in their worlds through their perfectly chosen words. They give us a chance to be present in the past, and to see our current world in its infinite variety. Too many of these kinds of anthologies keep us rooted in the West, and in the minds of white men. This collection seeks to champion long-overlooked poets. Thanks to the diverse array of poems here, you'll be able to travel to China, India, Pakistan, Jamaica and Sri Lanka – to name but a few – and celebrate festivals, religious (Easter and the Sikh Baisakhi) and national (Ireland's St Patrick's Day and Japan's *Midori no hi*) all from the comfort of your couch – or 'inward eye'.

The poems themselves come in all shapes and sizes. There are sonnets, ballads, limericks, odes, blank verses, rhyming couplets, haikus and cinquains, as well as extracts from epics and snapshots from plays, on subjects as disparate as tractor dreams, hippos and the sitcom *Friends*.

Each of these poems will be prefaced by a short introduction that will provide some background context – either about the poem's author, style or content – and the occasional anecdote.

This book has been compiled to be enjoyed by all the family. Until relatively recently, poems were never written with a particular age group in mind, and this anthology takes the view that the best poetry can work on different levels and is able to beguile children and adults alike. There are poems here for every spring day, and for every type of person to have their own favourite. I would love to hear from you which yours might be.

Allie Esiri

March

1 March • I am Taliesin • Anon.

The opening poem is in honour of St David's Day, the feast day of the Welsh patron saint who is celebrated every 1 March. These lines, thought to have been composed in the thirteenth century, have been passed down through generations as part of an ancient oral tradition and introduce us to the legendary and much-mythologized Welsh bard Taliesin.

I am Taliesin. I sing perfect metre,
Which will last to the end of the world.
My patron is Elphin . . .

I know why there is an echo in a hollow;
Why silver gleams; why breath is black; why liver is
  bloody;
Why a cow has horns; why a woman is affectionate;
Why milk is white; why holly is green;
Why a kid is bearded; why the cow-parsnip is hollow;
Why brine is salt; why ale is bitter;
Why the linnet is green and berries red;
Why a cuckoo complains; why it sings;
I know where the cuckoos of summer are in winter.
I know what beasts there are at the bottom of the sea;
How many spears in battle; how may drops in a shower;
Why a river drowned Pharaoh's people;
Why fishes have scales.
Why a white swan has black feet . . .

I have been a blue salmon,
I have been a dog, a stag, a roebuck on the mountain,
A stock, a spade, an axe in the hand,
A stallion, a bull, a buck,
I was reaped and placed in an oven;
I fell to the ground when I was being roasted
And a hen swallowed me.
For nine nights was I in her crop.
I have been dead, I have been alive.
I am Taliesin.

1 March • *from* Under Milk Wood • Dylan Thomas

Dylan Thomas, who was one of Wales's finest twentieth-century poets, wrote the following lines as part of his celebrated radio play *Under Milk Wood.*

Every morning when I wake,
Dear Lord, a little prayer I make,
O please do keep Thy lovely eye
On all poor creatures born to die.

And every evening at sun-down
I ask a blessing on the town,
For whether we last the night or no
I'm sure is always touch-and-go.

We are not wholly bad or good
Who live our lives under Milk Wood,
And Thou, I know, wilt be the first
To see our best side, not our worst.

O let us see another day!
Bless us this holy night, I pray,
And to the sun we all will bow
And say goodbye – but just for now!

2 March • The Bright Field • R. S. Thomas

R. S. Thomas was another proudly Welsh poet. A clergyman for much of his life, his poems are often spiritual in nature, and he frequently makes reference to Bible stories, as he does here with Moses and the burning bush. This poem is about how we live in the present moment. If life is not about the past or future, then it is about finding the right to look at the things directly in front of us, now.

I have seen the sun break through
to illuminate a small field
for a while, and gone my way
and forgotten it. But that was the
pearl of great price, the one field that had
the treasure in it. I realize now
that I must give all that I have
to possess it. Life is not hurrying

on to a receding future, nor hankering after
an imagined past. It is the turning
aside like Moses to the miracle
of the lit bush, to a brightness
that seemed as transitory as your youth
once, but is the eternity that awaits you.

2 March • March • Anon.

This traditional and simple rhyme hails originally from Northumberland. The strange word 'yeans' is from the local dialect, and means 'gives birth to'. The month of March is here described as a time in which new life springs forth – lambs frolic and thorns bloom into roses – but also a period in which the wind can be bitter and strong enough to blow through to the core of an ox's horn.

March yeans the lammie
 And buds the thorn,
And blows through the flint
 Of an ox's horn.

3 March • Anger Against Beasts • Wendell Berry

Today is World Wildlife Day. In this short yet visceral poem, the prolific American writer, philosopher, environmental activist – and farmer – Wendell Berry laments the unnatural and senseless acts of violence which humans inflict on animals.

The hook of adrenalin shoves
into the blood. Man's will,
long skilled to kill or have
its way, would drive the beast
against nature, transcend
the impossible in simple fury.
The blow falls like a dead seed.
It is defeat for beasts
do not pardon, but heal or die
in the absence of the past.
The blow survives in the man.
His triumph is a wound. Spent,
he must wait the slow
unalterable forgiveness of time.

3 March • Dear March – Come In • Emily Dickinson

This poem observes the paradox of the seasons: Emily Dickinson both praises and blames March for its beauty and its brevity.

Dear March – Come in –
How glad I am –
I hoped for you before –
Put down your Hat –
You must have walked –
How out of Breath you are –
Dear March, how are you, and the Rest –
Did you leave Nature well –
Oh March, Come right upstairs with me –
I have so much to tell –

I got your Letter, and the Birds –
The Maples never knew that you were coming – till I called
I declare – how Red their Faces grew –
But March, forgive me – and
All those Hills you left for me to Hue –
There was no Purple suitable –
You took it all with you –

Who knocks? That April –
Lock the Door –
I will not be pursued –
He stayed away a Year to call
When I am occupied –
But trifles look so trivial
As soon as you have come

That Blame is just as dear as Praise
And Praise as mere as Blame –

4 March • Holi • Chrissie Gittins

Holi is a Hindu festival that falls at this time of year. It is known as the 'Festival of Colours'. To mark the triumph of good (spring) over evil (winter), festival-goers brightly colour one another with handfuls of paints and dyed water balloons. Chrissie Gittins's poem imagines a language being made out of the colourful marks of the festival.

A splodge of purple on your neck
and you can feel the temperature rising.

A rub of brown on your cheek
and your friend is your friend for ever.

A cloud of red above your head
and your feet start itching to dance.

A scatter of yellow on your shirt
and your enemy is now your friend.

A blotch of blue on your nose
and the winter is soon forgotten.

A bucket of black down your back
and you are ready to beat the drum.

A stream of orange in the air
and your heart begins to surge.

A smear of pink on your forehead
and your misdeeds fade away.

A dusting of green on your eyelashes –
spring is surely on its way.

4 March • A Date with Spring • John Agard

This poem is a first-person monologue from the perspective of the tree itself, imagining the end of winter as a time where the tree prepares to get dressed ready for a 'date' with the new season – spring.

Got a date with spring
Got to look me best.
Of all the trees
I'll be the smartest dressed.

Perfumed breeze
behind me ear.
Pollen accessories
all in place.

Raindrop moisturizer
for me face.
Sunlight tints
to spruce up the hair.

What's the good of being a tree
if you can't flaunt your beauty?

Winter, I was naked
Exposed as can be.
Me wardrobe took off
with the wind.

Life was a frosty slumber.
Now, spring, here I come.
Can't wait to slip in
to me little green number.

5 March • The River in March • Ted Hughes

Ted Hughes was one of the greatest British poets of the twentieth century, and was poet laureate from 1984 until his death in 1998. He is mainly known for his nature poetry, often in deceptively plain language, and his poems show a great respect for the natural world.

Now the river is rich, but her voice is low.
It is her Mighty Majesty the sea
Travelling among the villages incognito.

Now the river is poor. No song, just a thin mad whisper.
The winter floods have ruined her.
She squats between draggled banks, fingering her rags
    and rubbish.

And now the river is rich. A deep choir.
It is the lofty clouds, that work in heaven,
Going on their holiday to the sea.

The river is poor again. All her bones are showing.
Through a dry wig of bleached flotsam she peers up
    ashamed
From her slum of sticks.

Now the river is rich, collecting shawls and minerals.
Rain brought fatness, but she takes ninety-nine percent
Leaving the fields just one percent to survive on.

And now she is poor. Now she is East wind sick.
She huddles in holes and corners. The brassy sun gives
her a headache.
She has lost all her fish. And she shivers.

But now once more she is rich. She is viewing her lands.
A hoard of king-cups spills from her folds, it blazes, it
cannot be hidden.
A salmon, a sow of solid silver,

Bulges to glimpse it.

5 March • Spring • Gerard Manley Hopkins

This sonnet begins by describing the beautiful qualities of spring, before comparing it to the Garden of Eden.

Nothing is so beautiful as Spring –
  When weeds, in wheels, shoot long and lovely and lush;
  Thrush's eggs look little low heavens, and thrush
Through the echoing timber does so rinse and wring
The ear, it strikes like lightnings to hear him sing;
  The glassy peartree leaves and blooms, they brush
  The descending blue; that blue is all in a rush
With richness; the racing lambs too have fair their fling.

What is all this juice and all this joy?
  A strain of the earth's sweet being in the beginning
In Eden garden. – Have, get, before it cloy,
  Before it cloud, Christ, lord, and sour with sinning,
Innocent mind and Mayday in girl and boy,
  Most, O maid's child, thy choice and worthy the winning.

6 March • Young Lambs • John Clare

We measure the seasons through a cycle of events. With the approach of spring, the season of new life, we see the arrival of young farmyard animals. John Clare celebrates the coming season with the lightness of his rhymes in this poem about lambs. Even in relating this jubilant display of life, however, Clare's poem seems drawn to the dark imagery of death.

The spring is coming by a many signs;
    The trays are up, the hedges broken down,
That fenced the haystack, and the remnant shines
    Like some old antique fragment weathered brown.
And where suns peep, in every sheltered place,
    The little early buttercups unfold
A glittering star or two – till many trace
    The edges of the blackthorn clumps in gold.
And then a little lamb bolts up behind
    The hill and wags his tail to meet the yoe,
And then another, sheltered from the wind,
    Lies all his length as dead – and lets me go
Close by and never stirs, but beaking lies,
    With legs stretched out as though he could not rise.

6 March • To My Sister • William Wordsworth

Like Ted Hughes and John Clare, and an inspiration to them both, William Wordsworth was a great poet of nature. And, like Hughes, he was also poet laureate. This poem is a celebration of taking the time to enjoy a beautiful day, away from work and responsibilities.

It is the first mild day of March:
Each minute sweeter than before,
The red-breast sings from the tall larch
That stands beside our door.

There is a blessing in the air,
Which seems a sense of joy to yield
To the bare trees, and mountains bare,
And grass in the green field.

My Sister! ('tis a wish of mine)
Now that our morning meal is done,
Make haste, your morning task resign;
Come forth and feel the sun.

Edward will come with you – and, pray,
Put on with speed your woodland dress,
And bring no book: for this one day
We'll give to idleness.

No joyless forms shall regulate
Our living Calendar:
We from today, my friend, will date
The opening of the year.

Love, now an universal birth,
From heart to heart is stealing,
From earth to man, from man to earth –
It is the hour of feeling.

One moment now may give us more
Than fifty years of reason;
Our minds shall drink at every pore
The spirit of the season.

Some silent laws our hearts will make,
Which they shall long obey:
We for the year to come may take
Our temper from today.

And from the blessed power that rolls
About, below, above,
We'll frame the measure of our souls:
They shall be tuned to love.

Then come, my sister! come, I pray,
With speed put on your woodland dress,
And bring no book: for this one day
We'll give to idleness.

7 March • But These Things Also • Edward Thomas

Edward Thomas wrote this poem in 1915, and its message carries memories of the great losses that occurred in the winter of 1914 during the First World War.

But these things also are Spring's—
On banks by the roadside the grass
Long-dead that is greyer now
Than all the Winter it was;

The shell of a little snail bleached
In the grass; chip of flint, and mite
Of chalk; and the small birds' dung
In splashes of purest white:

All the white things a man mistakes
For earliest violets
Who seeks through Winter's ruins
Something to pay Winter's debts,

While the North blows, and starling flocks
By chattering on and on
Keep their spirits up in the mist,
And Spring's here, Winter's not gone.

7 March • The Sound Collector • Roger McGough

On 7 March 1876, the inventor Alexander Graham Bell patented an object which changed the human experience of sound and communication forever: the telephone. This poem by Roger McGough imagines everyday sounds as objects which might be put into a bag and carried away.

A stranger called this morning
Dressed all in black and grey
Put every sound into a bag
And carried them away

The whistling of the kettle
The turning of the lock
The purring of the kitten
The ticking of the clock

The popping of the toaster
The crunching of the flakes
When you spread the marmalade
The scraping noise it makes

The hissing of the frying pan
The ticking of the grill
The bubbling of the bathtub
As it starts to fill

The drumming of the raindrops
On the windowpane
When you do the washing-up
The gurgle of the drain

The crying of the baby
The squeaking of the chair
The swishing of the curtain
The creaking of the stair

A stranger called this morning
He didn't leave his name
Left us only silence
Life will never be the same

8 March • Warning • Jenny Joseph

8 March is International Women's Day, a celebration of the political, social and cultural achievements of women everywhere. The day exists as a symbol of the victories made so far in the struggle for gender equality, although its existence is also a sign that equality has not yet been gained. Jenny Joseph's warm and comical poem makes fun of the rules that seem to govern being a woman in modern society, and it represents a quiet but important act of female defiance.

When I am an old woman I shall wear purple
With a red hat which doesn't go, and doesn't suit me.
And I shall spend my pension on brandy and summer
 gloves
And satin sandals, and say we've no money for butter.
I shall sit down on the pavement when I'm tired
And gobble up samples in shops and press alarm bells
And run my stick along the public railings
And make up for the sobriety of my youth.
I shall go out in my slippers in the rain
And pick the flowers in other people's gardens
And learn to spit.

You can wear terrible shirts and grow more fat
And eat three pounds of sausages at a go
Or only bread and pickle for a week
And hoard pens and pencils and beermats and things in boxes.

But now we must have clothes that keep us dry
And pay our rent and not swear in the street
And set a good example for the children.
We must have friends to dinner and read the papers.

But maybe I ought to practise a little now?
So people who know me are not too shocked and surprised
When suddenly I am old, and start to wear purple.

8 March • Phenomenal Woman • Maya Angelou

Here we have another great, rousing poem that celebrates womanhood in all its variety. Much like Jenny Joseph's 'Warning', this piece encourages women to take pride in who they are, and to reject dated, restrictive societal expectations about how a woman should be. It is one of countless inspiring poems by Maya Angelou – the pioneering African American writer who was a tireless champion of civil rights, women's rights, and by all accounts, a 'phenomenal woman' herself.

Pretty women wonder where my secret lies.
I'm not cute or built to suit a fashion model's size
But when I start to tell them,
They think I'm telling lies.
I say,
It's in the reach of my arms,
The span of my hips,
The stride of my step,
The curl of my lips.
I'm a woman
Phenomenally.
Phenomenal woman,
That's me.

I walk into a room
Just as cool as you please,
And to a man,
The fellows stand or
Fall down on their knees.
Then they swarm around me,
A hive of honey bees.
I say,
It's the fire in my eyes,
And the flash of my teeth,
The swing in my waist,
And the joy in my feet.
I'm a woman
Phenomenally.
Phenomenal woman,
That's me.

Men themselves have wondered
What they see in me.
They try so much
But they can't touch
My inner mystery.
When I try to show them,
They say they still can't see.
I say,
It's in the arch of my back,
The sun of my smile,
The ride of my breasts,
The grace of my style.
I'm a woman
Phenomenally.
Phenomenal woman,
That's me.

Now you understand
Just why my head's not bowed.
I don't shout or jump about
Or have to talk real loud.
When you see me passing,
It ought to make you proud.
I say,
It's in the click of my heels,
The bend of my hair,
the palm of my hand,
The need for my care.
'Cause I'm a woman
Phenomenally.
Phenomenal woman,
That's me.

9 March • The Battle of the Sexes • Liz Brownlee

While International Women's Day takes place annually on 8 March, its call for equality continues to resonate throughout the year and in many different gestures, some big, some small. In 1973, the male ex-tennis champion Bobby Riggs challenged the great female tennis champion Billie Jean King to a tennis match, asserting that she could not, as a woman, beat him. In front of a TV audience of over 45 million, in a match that came to be known as 'The Battle of the Sexes', Billie Jean King won. Although this match did not happen on International Women's Day, the spirit of what the day commemorates is captured in this poem by Liz Brownlee.

Bobby Riggs, tennis champ,
said a woman couldn't
beat a man . . .

Billie Jean King, tennis champ,
in three straight sets, showed
a woman can.

9 March • 'Hope' is the Thing with Feathers • Emily Dickinson

In this poem, Emily Dickinson imagines hope to be a bird that lives in the soul, singing eternally. Dickinson's reassuring poem notes with wonder that while hope has sustained the speaker through the darkest of times, it has never required anything in return.

'Hope' is the thing with feathers –
That perches in the soul –
And sings the tune without the words –
And never stops – at all –

And sweetest – in the Gale – is heard –
And sore must be the storm –
That could abash the little Bird
That kept so many warm –

I've heard it in the chillest land –
And on the strangest Sea –
Yet, never, in Extremity,
It asked a crumb – of Me.

10 March • Remember • Christina Rossetti

Christina Rossetti is associated with the Pre-Raphaelite movement, which was founded by her brother Dante Gabriel Rossetti, along with the painters William Holman Hunt and John Everett Millais. The Pre-Raphaelites rejected the major recent trends in Victorian art in favour of an older inspiration. Christina Rossetti's most well-known work is the poem 'In the Bleak Midwinter', which was set to music by Gustav Holst and is still performed as a Christmas carol today. In this poem, which is in the fourteen-line sonnet form, a lover imagines how she will be remembered once she has passed away.

Remember me when I am gone away,
  Gone far away into the silent land;
  When you can no more hold me by the hand,
Nor I half turn to go, yet turning stay.
Remember me when no more day by day
  You tell me of our future that you planned:
  Only remember me; you understand
It will be late to counsel then or pray.
Yet if you should forget me for a while
  And afterwards remember, do not grieve:
  For if the darkness and corruption leave
  A vestige of the thoughts that once I had,
Better by far you should forget and smile
  Than that you should remember and be sad.

10 March • Knocks on the Door • Maram al-Massri, translated by Khaled Mattawa

Loneliness is here likened to dust. The poem ends with the suggestion that the emotions we show the world are perhaps not always those which we truly feel.

Knocks on the door.
Who?
I sweep the dust of my loneliness
under the rug.
I arrange a smile
and open.

11 March • Green Rain • Mary Webb

Mary Webb's novels and poems usually focus on the landscape of her native Shropshire. Her poems in particular are snapshot images of the natural world, and in this poem the sense of peace and stillness she feels while walking through woodlands gives the impression that even the rain might hang in the air and cease to move.

Into the scented woods we'll go,
And see the blackthorn swim in snow.
High above, in the budding leaves,
A brooding dove awakes and grieves;
The glades with mingled music stir,
And wildly laughs the woodpecker.
When blackthorn petals pearl the breeze,
There are the twisted hawthorn trees
Thick-set with buds, as clear and pale
As golden water or green hail –
As if a storm of rain had stood
Enchanted in the thorny wood,
And, hearing fairy voices call,
Hung poised, forgetting how to fall.

11 March • Prior Knowledge • Carol Ann Duffy

Do you think Prior Knowledge is a real boy, or an imaginary friend? Although we all sometimes wish that we could have all the answers, this poem can be interpreted as a warning that knowledge can come at a price.

Prior Knowledge was a strange boy.
He had sad green eyes.
He always seemed to know when I was telling lies.

We were friends for a summer.
Prior got out his knife
and mixed our bloods so we'd be brothers for life.

You'll be rich, he said, and famous;
but I must die.
Then brave, clever Prior began to cry.

He knew so much.
he knew the day before
I'd drop a jamjar full of frogspawn on the kitchen floor.

He knew there were wasps
in the gardening gloves.
He knew the name of the girl I'd grow up to love.

The day he died
he knew there would be
a wind shaking conkers from the horse-chestnut tree;

and an aimless child
singing down Prior's street,
with bright red sandals on her skipping feet.

12 March • Tarantella • Hilaire Belloc

A 'tarantella' is a fast, upbeat dance that is supposed to mimic the feverish, frenzied effect of a spider bite – it literally means 'tarantula' in Italian – or of falling in love. This poem, with its repetitions and one-word lines, captures the swift and relentless rhythm of the dance being described.

Do you remember an Inn,
Miranda?
Do you remember an Inn?
And the tedding and the spreading
Of the straw for a bedding,
And the fleas that tease in the High Pyrenees,
And the wine that tasted of tar?
And the cheers and the jeers of the young muleteers
(Under the vine of the dark veranda)?
Do you remember an Inn, Miranda,
Do you remember an Inn?
And the cheers and the jeers of the young muleteers
Who hadn't got a penny,
And who weren't paying any,
And the hammer at the doors and the din?
And the hip! hop! hap!
Of the clap
Of the hands to the swirl and the twirl
Of the girl gone chancing,
Glancing,
Dancing,
Backing and advancing,
Snapping of the clapper to the spin

Out and in –
And the ting, tong, tang of the guitar!
Do you remember an Inn,
Miranda?
Do you remember an Inn?
Never more;
Miranda,
Never more.
Only the high peaks hoar;
And Aragon a torrent at the door.
No sound
In the walls of the halls where falls
The tread
Of the feet of the dead to the ground,
No sound:
But the boom
Of the far waterfall like doom.

12 March • *from* The Lady of Shalott • Alfred, Lord Tennyson

This epic narrative poem by Alfred, Lord Tennyson takes its inspiration from a thirteenth-century Italian romance and tales of the mythical King Arthur. These wonderfully evocative opening verses introduce us to the bucolic idyll of Camelot, where the beguiling and mysterious Lady of Shalott remains cloistered inside her island castle after a strange curse prevents her from directly looking at the outside world.

On either side the river lie
Long fields of barley and of rye,
That clothe the wold and meet the sky;
And thro' the field the road runs by
        To many-tower'd Camelot;
And up and down the people go,
Gazing where the lilies blow
Round an island there below,
        The island of Shalott.

Willows whiten, aspens quiver,
Little breezes dusk and shiver
Thro' the wave that runs for ever
By the island in the river
        Flowing down to Camelot.
Four gray walls, and four gray towers,
Overlook a space of flowers,
And the silent isle imbowers
        The Lady of Shalott.

By the margin, willow-veil'd,
Slide the heavy barges trail'd
By slow horses; and unhail'd
The shallop flitteth silken-sail'd
Skimming down to Camelot:
But who hath seen her wave her hand?
Or at the casement seen her stand?
Or is she known in all the land,
The Lady of Shalott?

Only reapers, reaping early
In among the bearded barley,
Hear a song that echoes cheerly
From the river winding clearly,
Down to tower'd Camelot:
And by the moon the reaper weary,
Piling sheaves in uplands airy,
Listening, whispers, ''Tis the fairy
Lady of Shalott.'

13 March • Seasons of the Heart • Linton Kwesi Johnson

The Jamaican-born dub poet Linton Kwesi Johnson is one of the UK's most prominent and celebrated contemporary writers. While many of his poems have a political resonance, this piece is more grounded in nature and shared human experiences of love and ageing. Here he beautifully equates life's ups and downs with the inevitable changing of the seasons, and gently implores us to make the most of the 'springtime of our days' before we retreat into the 'winter of our minds'.

Beguiled
by blue moon
O enchanting light

we lost our way
like lovers sometimes do
searching wide-eyed
for wild flowers
in the 'fragrant forest of the night'

now memories
slowly drift on by
like grey clouds
against the somber winter sky
and all our yesterdays are now become
the springtime of our days

life is the greatest teacher
love is the lesson to be learnt
like how the heart's seasons shift
how the sweet smelling blossoms of spring
are soon become the icy arrows of winter's sting
how spring intoxicated by the sun
now throws off her green gown
and summer's golden smile is soon become
the frown of autumn's brown
how passions spent we droop like sapless vines
In the winter of our minds

13 March • Lochinvar • Sir Walter Scott

Sir Walter Scott was a nineteenth-century historical novelist and poet who was much admired during his lifetime. Much of his work centred upon stories of adventure and gallantry that play out in his native Scottish countryside – and this poem is no different. Set in medieval times, it follows the dashing hero Lochinvar as he gatecrashes a marital feast and steals away the bride from her dastardly husband-to-be with little more than 'one touch to her hand, and one word in her ear'.

O young Lochinvar is come out of the west,
Through all the wide Border his steed was the best;
And save his good broadsword he weapons had none,
He rode all unarm'd, and he rode all alone.
So faithful in love, and so dauntless in war,
There never was knight like the young Lochinvar.

He staid not for brake, and he stopp'd not for stone,
He swam the Eske river where ford there was none;
But ere he alighted at Netherby gate,
The bride had consented, the gallant came late:
For a laggard in love, and a dastard in war,
Was to wed the fair Ellen of brave Lochinvar.

So boldly he enter'd the Netherby Hall,
Among bride's-men, and kinsmen, and brothers and all:
Then spoke the bride's father, his hand on his sword,
(For the poor craven bridegroom said never a word,)
'O come ye in peace here, or come ye in war,
Or to dance at our bridal, young Lord Lochinvar?'

'I long woo'd your daughter, my suit you denied;—
Love swells like the Solway, but ebbs like its tide—
And now I am come, with this lost love of mine,
To lead but one measure, drink one cup of wine.
There are maidens in Scotland more lovely by far,
That would gladly be bride to the young Lochinvar.'

The bride kiss'd the goblet: the knight took it up,
He quaff'd off the wine, and he threw down the cup.
She look'd down to blush, and she look'd up to sigh,
With a smile on her lips and a tear in her eye.
He took her soft hand, ere her mother could bar,—
'Now tread we a measure!' said young Lochinvar.

So stately his form, and so lovely her face,
That never a hall such a galliard did grace;
While her mother did fret, and her father did fume,
And the bridegroom stood dangling his bonnet and plume;
And the bride-maidens whisper'd, ''Twere better by far
To have match'd our fair cousin with young Lochinvar.'

One touch to her hand, and one word in her ear,
When they reach'd the hall-door, and the charger stood near;
So light to the croupe the fair lady he swung,
So light to the saddle before her he sprung!
'She is won! we are gone, over bank, bush, and scaur;
They'll have fleet steeds that follow,' quoth young Lochinvar.

There was mounting 'mong Graemes of the Netherby clan;
Forsters, Fenwicks, and Musgraves, they rode and they ran:
There was racing and chasing on Cannobie Lee,
But the lost bride of Netherby ne'er did they see.
So daring in love, and so dauntless in war,
Have ye e'er heard of gallant like young Lochinvar?

14 March • Mothering Sunday • George Hare Leonard

Mother's Day falls in March in the United Kingdom. The day celebrates the selfless and essential role that mothers play in families and society alike. In times past, maids and servants were allowed to take the day off to see their mothers and go to church. They would take with them cakes and other treats for their mothers – like the specially baked wheaten cake in this poem.

It is the day of all the year,
Of all the year the one day,
When I shall see my Mother dear
  And bring her cheer,
A-Mothering on Sunday.

And now to fetch my wheaten cake,
To fetch it from the baker,
He promised me, for Mother's sake,
  The best he'd bake
For me to fetch and take her.

Well have I known, as I went by
One hollow lane, that none day
I'd fail to find – for all they're shy –
  Where violets lie,
As I went home on Sunday.

My sister Jane is waiting-maid
Along with Squire's lady;
And year by year her part she's played,
  And home she stayed
To get the dinner ready.

For Mother'll come to Church, you'll see –
Of all the year it's the day –
'The one,' she'll say, 'that's made for me.'
  And so it be:
It's every Mother's free day.

The boys will all come home from town,
Not one will miss that one day;
And every maid will bustle down
  To show her gown,
A-Mothering on Sunday.

It is the day of all the year,
Of all the year the one day;
And here come I, my Mother dear,
  And bring you cheer,
A-Mothering on Sunday.

14 March • Human Affection • Stevie Smith

Here is another one for Mother's Day, from British poet Stevie Smith. It is an illustration of how even one scene, one image, can convey a depth of emotion in poetry.

Mother, I love you so.
Said the child, I love you more than I know.
She laid her head on her mother's arm,
And the love between them kept them warm.

15 March • To Daffodils • Robert Herrick

Robert Herrick was one of the seventeenth-century 'Cavalier poets', so named because they supported King Charles during the English Civil War (Charles was eventually executed). Herrick wrote well over two thousand poems in his life, many of which were inspired by the Latin expression *carpe diem* – 'seize the day'. A 'carpe diem' poem is one that focuses on the shortness of life and thus on the importance of enjoying every present moment.

Fair daffodils, we weep to see
  You haste away so soon;
As yet the early-rising sun
  Has not attain'd his noon.
    Stay, stay,
  Until the hasting day
    Has run
  But to the evensong;
And, having prayed together, we
  Will go with you along.

We have short time to stay, as you,
  We have as short a spring;
As quick a growth to meet decay,
  As you, or anything.
    We die,
  As your hours do, and dry
    Away,
  Like to the summer's rain;
Or as the pearls of morning's dew,
  Ne'er to be found again.

15 March • *from* Julius Caesar • William Shakespeare

In the Roman calendar, the Ides of March is a date which corresponds to 15 March in our calendar – each month had an Ides which signified, roughly, its midpoint. On the Ides of March 44 BC, Julius Caesar, the great statesman and general, was assassinated in the Roman senate. These lines come from the famous scene in William Shakespeare's play *Julius Caesar*, in which a soothsayer (or fortune teller) warns Caesar of imminent danger. Perhaps if they had offered some more information than just the rather cryptic 'beware', Caesar would have been more inclined to heed their advice. As it is, Caesar joins Macbeth and Antony in the pantheon of Shakespeare characters who should have listened more carefully to their prophecies.

CAESAR
Who is it in the press that calls on me?
I hear a tongue, shriller than all the music,
Cry 'Caesar!' Speak; Caesar is turn'd to hear.
SOOTHSAYER
Beware the Ides of March.
CAESAR
What man is that?
BRUTUS
A soothsayer bids you beware the Ides of March.
CAESAR
Set him before me; let me see his face.
CASSIUS
Fellow, come from the throng; look upon Caesar.

CAESAR

What say'st thou to me now? Speak once again.

SOOTHSAYER

Beware the Ides of March.

CAESAR

He is a dreamer; let us leave him: pass.

16 March • Go and Catch a Falling Star • John Donne

This poem at first hides its theme. It asks the reader to perform impossible tasks relating to mythological things and beings, and to go on lifelong travels. Only at the end of the second stanza is it revealed that these impossibilities are being used as a cynical and rather bitter comparison to another ostensibly unfeasible endeavour: finding a true and fair woman.

Go and catch a falling star,
  Get with child a mandrake root,
Tell me where all past years are,
  Or who cleft the Devil's foot;
Teach me to hear mermaids singing,
Or to keep off envy's stinging,
      And find
      What wind
Serves to advance an honest mind.

If thou be'st born to strange sights,
  Things invisible to see,
Ride ten thousand days and nights
  Till Age snow white hairs on thee;
Thou, when thou return'st, wilt tell me,
All strange wonders that befell thee,
      And swear,
      No where
Lives a woman true and fair.

If thou find'st one, let me know;
  Such a pilgrimage were sweet.
Yet do not; I would not go,
  Though at next door we might meet.
Though she were true when you met her,
And last, till you write your letter,
        Yet she
        Will be
False, ere I come, to two or three.

16 March • Toad • Norman MacCaig

The Scottish poet Norman MacCaig often wrote about the natural world and animals, such as the toad in this poem. This poem's positivity is a refreshing way to look at a creature that is often regarded as ugly, or even scary.

Stop looking like a purse. How could a purse
Squeeze under the rickety door and sit,
Full of satisfaction in a man's house?

You clamber towards me on your four corners –
Right hand, left foot, left hand, right foot.

I love you for being a toad,
For crawling like a Japanese wrestler,
And for not being frightened.

I put you in my purse hand, not shutting it,
And set you down outside directly under
Every star.

A jewel in your head? Toad,
You've put one in mine,
A tiny radiance in a dark place.

17 March • Ich Am of Irlaunde • Anon.

17 March is St Patrick's Day. As St Patrick is the patron saint of Ireland, it is also a day on which people celebrate the culture and history of the Emerald Isle. St Patrick's Day is thought to be the most widely celebrated national festival in the world. The song 'Ich Am of Irlaunde' is a traditional medieval poem originating in around the year 1300. Reading and making sense of a poem like this can require some concentration, but it is also rewarding; it teaches us about the history of the English language itself.

Ich am of Irlaunde,
And of the holy londe
  Of Irlande.

Gode sire, pray ich thee,
For of sainte charite,
Come an daunce wit me
  In Irlaunde.

Translation

I am of Ireland,
and of the holy realm
of Ireland.

Good sir, I pray thee:
for the sake of holy charity,
come and dance with me
in Ireland.

17 March • He Wishes for the Cloths of Heaven • W. B. Yeats

W. B. Yeats is one of Ireland's most revered poets and is remembered as one of the key figures of the twentieth-century literary movement known as modernism. Although he accomplished many great things in his career – not least winning the Nobel Prize in Literature in 1923 – he would have probably traded all his achievements for a reciprocation of his love for his muse. This is one of his shortest, and most heartbreaking, poems written to Maud Gonne, who sadly never agreed to marry him despite numerous proposals – and poems!

Had I the heavens' embroidered cloths,
Enwrought with golden and silver light,
The blue and the dim and the dark cloths
Of night and light and the half-light,
I would spread the cloths under your feet:
But I, being poor, have only my dreams;
I have spread my dreams under your feet;
Tread softly because you tread on my dreams.

18 March • Spring Snow • John Foster

The cinquain (a poem of five lines with two, four, six, eight and two syllables on each line) is the perfect format for John Foster's poem which concentrates on the fleeting beauty of snowflakes.

Snowflakes
Slip from the sky
Like soft white butterflies,
Brush the trees with their flimsy wings,
Vanish.

18 March • Meeting at Night • Robert Browning

This love poem was written around 1845, when Robert Browning was courting his future wife, the poet Elizabeth Barrett. The simple narrative of the poem focuses less on the meeting of the lovers, and more on the journey leading up to that meeting. We do not have much access to the narrator's thoughts, but through the images of the sea and the landscape he passes, we experience a sense of mounting anticipation.

The grey sea and the long black land;
And the yellow half-moon large and low;
And the startled little waves that leap
In fiery ringlets from their sleep,
As I gain the cove with pushing prow,
And quench its speed i' the slushy sand.

Then a mile of warm sea-scented beach;
Three fields to cross till a farm appears;
A tap at the pane, the quick sharp scratch
And blue spurt of a lighted match,
And a voice less loud, through joys and fears,
Than the two hearts beating each to each!

19 March • Historical Associations • Robert Louis Stevenson

Among Robert Louis Stevenson's most famous works today are the novels *Treasure Island* and *Dr Jekyll and Mr Hyde*. He was also noted for his wonderful volume of poetry, *A Child's Garden of Verses*. This imaginative poem is a series of reflections, or jumps between thoughts, as a child, playing with his uncle, travels far and wide through geography and history, and still gets home in time for tea.

Dear Uncle Jim, this garden ground
That now you smoke your pipe around,
Has seen immortal actions done
And valiant battles lost and won.

Here we had best on tip-toe tread,
While I for safety march ahead,
For this is that enchanted ground
Where all who loiter slumber sound.

Here is the sea, here is the sand,
Here is simple Shepherd's Land,
Here are the fairy hollyhocks,
And there are Ali Baba's rocks.

But yonder, see! apart and high,
Frozen Siberia lies; where I,
With Robert Bruce and William Tell,
Was bound by an enchanter's spell.

There, then, awhile in chains we lay,
In wintry dungeons, far from day;
But ris'n at length, with might and main,
Our iron fetters burst in twain.

Then all the horns were blown in town;
And to the ramparts clanging down,
All the giants leaped to horse
And charged behind us through the gorse.

On we rode, the others and I,
Over the mountains blue, and by
The Silver River, the sounding sea
And the robber woods of Tartary.

A thousand miles we galloped fast,
And down the witches' lane we passed,
And rode amain, with brandished sword,
Up to the middle, through the ford.

Last we drew rein – a weary three –
Upon the lawn, in time for tea,
And from our steeds alighted down
Before the gates of Babylon.

19 March • Three Good Things • Jan Dean

This is a perfect poem to put under your pillow and read at day's end.

At day's end I remember
three good things.

Apples maybe – their skinshine smell
and soft froth of juice.

Water maybe – the pond in the park
dark and full of secret fish.

A mountain maybe – that I saw in a film,
or climbed last holiday,
and suddenly today it thundered up
into a playground game.
Or else an owl – I heard an owl today,
and I made bread.
My head is full of all these things,
it's hard to choose just three.

I let remembering fill me up
with all good things
so that good things will overflow
into my sleeping self,

and in the morning
good things will be waiting
when I wake.

20 March • A Morning Song • Eleanor Farjeon

Around 19–21 March is the vernal equinox, which is the start of spring. These words were written in 1931 by Eleanor Farjeon, but became well known as a hymn after they were set to a Gaelic tune.

Morning has broken
Like the first morning,
Blackbird has spoken
  Like the first bird.
Praise for the singing!
Praise for the morning!
Praise for them, springing
  From the first Word.

Sweet the rain's new fall,
Sunlit from heaven,
Like the first dewfall
  In the first hour.
Praise for the sweetness,
Of the wet garden,
Sprung in completeness
  From the first shower.

Mine is the sunlight!
Mine is the morning
Born of the one light
  Eden saw play.
Praise with elation,
Praise every morning
Spring's re-creation
  Of the new day!

20 March · *from* Pippa Passes · Robert Browning

This poem from Robert Browning's verse drama *Pippa Passes* is a poem about beginnings – about dew-pearled mornings and a year about to blossom. Pippa celebrates the simple wonders of nature, finding a connection between the snail resting on a thorn and the idea of God in heaven.

The year's at the spring
And day's at the morn;
Morning's at seven;
The hillside's dew-pearled;
The lark's on the wing;
The snail's on the thorn:
God's in His heaven—
All's right with the world!

21 March • Spring • Christina Rossetti

Spring is the season of life, birth and rebirth. But poetry often finds reminders of things in their opposites, and even life can serve to be a reminder of death. In Rossetti's simple song of spring, the poet cannot resist seeing the season of spring as a time 'that passes by' all too soon.

Frost-locked all the winter,
Seeds, and roots, and stones of fruits,
What shall make their sap ascend
That they may put forth shoots?
Tips of tender green,
Leaf, or blade, or sheath;
Telling of the hidden life
That breaks forth underneath,
Life nursed in its grave by Death.

Blows the thaw-wind pleasantly,
Drips the soaking rain,
By fits looks down the waking sun:
Young grass springs on the plain;
Young leaves clothe early hedgerow trees;
Seeds, and roots, and stones of fruits,
Swollen with sap put forth their shoots;
Curled-headed ferns sprout in the lane;
Birds sing and pair again.

There is no time like Spring,
When life's alive in everything,
Before new nestlings sing,
Before cleft swallows speed their journey back
Along the trackless track –
God guides their wing,
He spreads their table that they nothing lack, –
Before the daisy grows a common flower
Before the sun has power
To scorch the world up in his noontide hour.

There is no time like Spring,
Like Spring that passes by;
There is no life like Spring-life born to die,
Piercing the sod,
Clothing the uncouth clod,
Hatched in the nest,
Fledged on the windy bough,
Strong on the wing:
There is no time like Spring that passes by,
Now newly born, and now
Hastening to die.

21 March • Flowers and Moonlight on the Spring River • Yang-Ti, translated by Arthur Waley

The emperor Yang-Ti ruled the Sui Dynasty in China from 604 to his death in 618. Despite his infamous reputation as one of China's most cruel and tyrannical sovereigns, he was capable of writing such beautiful, meditative lines as these, which evoke the simultaneous radiance and transience of nature. Whether he was the best poet of his generation we'll never know, as Yang was known to execute any writers who he feared might be superior to him.

> The evening river is level and motionless –
> The spring colours just open to their full.
> Suddenly a wave carries the moon away
> And the tidal water comes with its freight of stars.

22 March • Spring • William Blake

William Blake's collection of poems, *Songs of Innocence and Experience*, is celebrated as a great experiment in poetry, where he offsets the plain songs of joy of 'Innocence' with the complicated reflections found in 'Experience'. But even in the simpler poems we find Blake playing around with rhythms, such as the three-syllable rhymed lines in this poem about spring.

Sound the Flute
Now it's mute.
Birds delight
Day and Night;
Nightingale
In the dale
Lark in Sky,
Merrily,
Merrily, Merrily, to welcome in the Year.

Little Boy,
Full of joy;
Little Girl,
Sweet and small;
Cock does crow,
So do you;
Merry voice,
Infant noise,
Merrily, Merrily, to welcome in the Year.

Little Lamb,
Here I am;
Come and lick
My white neck;
Let me pull
Your soft Wool;
Let me kiss
Your soft face:
Merrily, Merrily, we welcome in the Year.

22 March • The Trees • Philip Larkin

Philip Larkin's work was famously melancholy, yet this poem deals with an optimistic subject: the approach of spring.

The trees are coming into leaf
Like something almost being said;
The recent buds relax and spread,
Their greenness is a kind of grief.

Is it that they are born again
And we grow old? No, they die too.
Their yearly trick of looking new
Is written down in rings of grain.

Yet still the unresting castles thresh
In fullgrown thickness every May.
Last year is dead, they seem to say,
Begin afresh, afresh, afresh.

23 March • Sonnet 98 • William Shakespeare

Shakespeare's sonnets are carefully measured – each line must have ten syllables, which alternate in stresses, and there must be a total of fourteen lines. They are usually arranged into very particular rhyme schemes and end with a couplet, which offers a final thought of its own.

From you have I been absent in the spring,
When proud-pied April, dress'd in all his trim,
Hath put a spirit of youth in everything,
That heavy Saturn laugh'd, and leap'd with him.
Yet nor the lays of birds, nor the sweet smell
Of different flowers in odour and in hue,
Could make me any summer's story tell,
Or from their proud lap pluck them where they grew:
Nor did I wonder at the lily's white,
Nor praise the deep vermilion in the rose;
They were but sweet, but figures of delight,
Drawn after you – you pattern of all those.
  Yet seem'd it winter still, and, you away,
  As with your shadow I with these did play.

23 March • in Just- • E. E. Cummings

E. E. Cummings was an American poet. In his poetry, the layout of the text on the page is crucial in establishing its meaning: in this poem, the differing sentence lengths create a feeling of excitement and change.

in Just-
spring   when the world is mud-
luscious the little
lame balloonman

whistles   far   and wee

and eddieandbill come
running from marbles and
piracies and it's
spring

when the world is puddle-wonderful

the queer
old balloonman whistles
far   and   wee
and bettyandisbel come dancing

from hop-scotch and jump-rope and

it's
spring
and
        the

                goat-footed

balloonMan   whistles
far
and
wee

24 March • The Frog and the Nightingale • Vikram Seth

This powerful rhyming fable about a cunning frog and a gullible nightingale is by the acclaimed Indian novelist and poet, Vikram Seth. It is a cautionary tale, whose moral is to beware of the unscrupulous master and always to have self-belief.

Once upon a time a frog
Croaked away in Bingle Bog.
Every night from dusk to dawn
He croaked awn and awn and awn.
Other creatures loathed his voice,
But, alas, they had no choice,
And the crass cacophony
Blared out from the sumac tree
At whose foot the frog each night
Minstrelled on till morning night.

Neither stones nor prayers nor sticks,
Insults or complaints or bricks
Stilled the frog's determination
To display his heart's elation.
But one night a nightingale
In the moonlight cold and pale
Perched upon the sumac tree
Casting forth her melody.
Dumbstruck sat the gaping frog
And the whole admiring bog
Stared towards the sumac, rapt,

And, when she had ended, clapped.
Ducks had swum and herons waded
To her as she serenaded,
And a solitary loon
Wept beneath the summer moon.
Toads and teals and tiddlers, captured
By her voice, cheered on, enraptured:
'Bravo!' 'Too divine!' 'Encore!'
So the nightingale once more,
Quite unused to such applause,
Sang till dawn without a pause.

Next night when the nightingale
Shook her head and twitched her tail,
Closed an eye and fluffed a wing,
And had cleared her throat to sing
She was startled by a croak.
'Sorry – was that you who spoke?'
She enquired when the frog
Hopped towards her from the bog.
'Yes,' the frog replied. 'You see,
I'm the frog who owns this tree.
In this bog I've long been known
For my splendid baritone
And, of course, I wield my pen
For *Bog Trumpet* now and then.'

'Did you . . . did you like my song?'
'Not too bad – but far too long.
The technique was fine, of course,
But it lacked a certain force.'
'Oh!' the nightingale confessed,
Greatly flattered and impressed
That a critic of such note
Had discussed her art and throat:

'I don't think the song's divine.
But – oh, well – at least it's mine.'

'That's not much to boast about,'
Said the heartless frog. 'Without
Proper training such as I
– And few others – can supply.
You'll remain a mere beginner.
But with me you'll be a winner.'
'Dearest frog,' the nightingale
Breathed: 'This is a fairy tale –
And you are Mozart in disguise
Come to earth before my eyes.'

'Well, I charge a modest fee.'
'Oh!' 'But it won't hurt, you'll see.'
Now the nightingale, inspired,
Flushed with confidence, and fired
With both art and adoration,
Sang – and was a huge sensation.
Animals for miles around
Flocked towards the magic sound,
And the frog with great precision
Counted heads and charged admission.

Though next morning it was raining,
He began her vocal training.
'But I can't sing in this weather.'
'Come, my dear – we'll sing together.
Just put on your scarf and sash.
Koo-oh-ah! ko-ash! ko-ash!'
So the frog and nightingale
Journeyed up and down the scale
For six hours, till she was shivering
And her voice was hoarse and quivering.

Though subdued and sleep deprived,
In the night her throat revived,
And the sumac tree was bowed
With a breathless, titled crowd:
Owl of Sandwich, Duck of Kent,
Mallard and Milady Trent,
Martin Cardinal Mephisto,
And the Coot of Monte Cristo.
Ladies with tiaras glittering
In the interval sat twittering –
And the frog observed them glitter
With a joy both sweet and bitter.

Every day the frog who'd sold her
Songs for silver tried to scold her:
'You must practise even longer
Till your voice, like mine, grows stronger.
In the second song last night
You got nervous in mid-flight.
And, my dear, lay on more trills:
Audiences enjoy such frills.
You must make your public happier:
Give them something sharper, snappier.
We must aim for better billings.
You still owe me sixty shillings.'

Day by day the nightingale
Grew more sorrowful and pale.
Night on night her tired song
Zipped and trilled and bounced along,
Till the birds and beasts grew tired
At a voice so uninspired

And the ticket office gross
Crashed, and she grew more morose –
For her ears were now addicted
To applause quite unrestricted,
And to sing into the night
All alone gave no delight.

Now the frog puffed up with rage.
'Brainless bird – you're on the stage
Use your wits, and follow fashion.
Puff your lungs out with your passion.'
Trembling, terrified to fail,
Blind with tears, the nightingale
Heard him out in silence, tried,
Puffed up, burst a vein, and died.

Said the frog: 'I tried to teach her,
But she was a stupid creature –
Far too nervous, far too tense,
Far too prone to influence.
Well, poor bird – she should have known
That your song must be your own.
That's why I sing with panache:
"Koo-oh-ah! ko-ash! ko-ash!"
And the foghorn of the frog
Blared unrivalled through the bog.

24 March • The Knight's Tomb • Samuel Taylor Coleridge

Samuel Taylor Coleridge wrote 'The Knight's Tomb' in 1817, long after the days when valiant knights roamed England wielding swords. The poem is filled with images of England's past and its natural beauty, yet Coleridge was writing during the Industrial Revolution when these natural spaces seemed in great peril.

Where is the grave of Sir Arthur O'Kellyn?
Where may the grave of that good man be?—
By the side of a spring, on the breast of Helvellyn,
Under the twigs of a young birch tree!
The oak that in summer was sweet to hear,
And rustled its leaves in the fall of the year,
And whistled and roared in the winter alone,
Is gone,—and the birch in its stead is grown.—
The Knight's bones are dust,
And his good sword rust;—
His soul is with the saints, I trust.

25 March • Today • Billy Collins

Billy Collins is among the foremost American poets alive today and was the poet laureate of the United States from 2001 to 2003. This is an example of how a poem can surprise us, by taking us on a journey through a writer's thoughts and feelings, in a single sentence.

If ever there were a spring day so perfect,
so uplifted by a warm intermittent breeze

that it made you want to throw
open all the windows in the house

and unlatch the door to the canary's cage,
indeed, rip the little door from its jamb,

a day when the cool brick paths
and the garden bursting with peonies

seemed so etched in sunlight
that you felt like taking

a hammer to the glass paperweight
on the living room end table,

releasing the inhabitants
from their snow-covered cottage

so they could walk out,
holding hands and squinting

into this larger dome of blue and white,
well, today is just that kind of day.

25 March • In a Station of the Metro • Ezra Pound

For Ezra Pound, the visual image of a poem was closely linked to its meaning, and he insisted that this poem was printed in the striking layout shown below. It brings the presence of nature into the urban Parisian station – even here the springtime imagery of rainy woodlands and blossoms is discernible.

The apparition   of these faces   in the crowd   :
Petals   on a wet, black   bough   .

26 March • I Remember, I Remember • Thomas Hood

Thomas Hood was a Victorian poet who, like Christina Rossetti, was concerned with the powers of memory and remembering. Unlike Rossetti's 'Remember', Hood's poem is a lively celebration of memory right up until its final lines.

I remember, I remember,
The house where I was born,
The little window where the sun
Came peeping in at morn;
He never came a wink too soon,
Nor brought too long a day,
But now, I often wish the night
Had borne my breath away!

I remember, I remember,
The roses, red and white,
The violets, and the lily-cups,
Those flowers made of light!
The lilacs where the robin built,
And where my brother set
The laburnum on his birthday, –
The tree is living yet!

I remember, I remember,
Where I was used to swing,
And thought the air must rush as fresh
To swallows on the wing;
My spirit flew in feathers then,
That is so heavy now,
And summer pools could hardly cool
The fever on my brow!

I remember, I remember,
The fir trees dark and high;
I used to think their slender tops
Were close against the sky:
It was a childish ignorance,
But now 'tis little joy
To know I'm farther off from heav'n
Than when I was a boy.

26 March • A Donkey • Ted Hughes

Ted Hughes, who grew up in rural West Yorkshire, often wrote poems about animals. The repetition of 'I like' conveys an affection for all of the animal's bizarre features.

His face is what I like.
And his head, much too big for his body – a toy head,
A great, rabbit-eared, pantomime head,
And his friendly rabbit face,
His big, friendly, humorous eyes – which can turn
    wicked,
Long and devilish, when he lays his ears back.

But mostly he's comical – and that's what I like.
I like the joke he seems
Always just about to tell me. And the laugh,
The rusty, pump-house engine that cranks up laughter
From some long-ago, far off, laughter-less desert –

The dry, hideous guffaw
That makes his great teeth nearly fall out.

27 March • Ballad of the Bread Man • Charles Causley

Charles Causley was a twentieth-century Cornish writer. As popular among the celebrity poets of his day as he was with readers, he counted Siegfried Sassoon and Ted Hughes as close friends. The 'Ballad of the Bread Man' is a modernized telling of the life and death of Jesus. Even the three wise men appear, as a bishop, a general and an African leader. Though it begins in comic fashion, it ends on a very different tone, and the final stanza reveals Causley's own view of the modern attitude towards spiritual knowledge. Jesus returns from the dead, only to find that the public still has no interest in his message of peace and morality. Causley lived through the Second World War and may have had those experiences in mind.

Mary stood in the kitchen
  Baking a loaf of bread.
An angel flew in through the window.
  'We've a job for you,' he said.

'God in his big gold heaven
  Sitting in his big blue chair,
Wanted a mother for his little son.
  Suddenly saw you there.'

Mary shook and trembled,
  'It isn't true what you say.'
'Don't say that,' said the angel.
  'The baby's on its way.'

Joseph was in the workshop
  Planing a piece of wood.
'The old man's past it,' the neighbours said.
  'That girl's been up to no good.'

'And who was that elegant fellow,'
  They said, 'in the shiny gear?'
The things they said about Gabriel
  Were hardly fit to hear.

Mary never answered,
  Mary never replied.
She kept the information,
  Like the baby, safe inside.

It was the election winter.
  They went to vote in town.
When Mary found her time had come
  The hotels let her down.

The baby was born in an annexe
  Next to the local pub.
At midnight, a delegation
  Turned up from the Farmers' Club.

They talked about an explosion
  That made a hole in the sky,
Said they'd been sent to the Lamb and Flag
  To see God come down from on high.

A few days later a bishop
  And a five-star general were seen
With the head of an African country
  In a bullet-proof limousine.

'We've come,' they said, 'with tokens
For the little boy to choose.'
Told the tale about war and peace
In the television news.

After them came the soldiers
With rifle and bombs and gun,
Looking for enemies of the state.
The family had packed up and gone.

When they got back to the village
The neighbours said, to a man,
'That boy will never be one of us,
Though he does what he blessed well can.'

He went round to all the people
A paper crown on his head.
Here is some bread from my father.
Take, eat, he said.

Nobody seemed very hungry.
Nobody seemed to care.
Nobody saw the God in himself
Quietly standing there.

He finished up in the papers,
He came to a very bad end.
He was charged with bringing the living to life.
No man was that prisoner's friend.

There's only one kind of punishment
To fit that kind of crime.
They rigged a trial and shot him dead.
They were only just in time.

They lifted the young man by the leg,
  They lifted him by the arm,
They locked him in a cathedral
  In case he came to harm.

They stored him safe as water
  Under seven rocks.
One Sunday morning he burst out
  Like a jack-in-the-box.

Through the town he went walking.
  He showed them the holes in his head.
Now do you want any loaves? he cried.
  'Not today,' they said.

27 March • The Donkey • G. K. Chesterton

Like Charles Causley, G. K. Chesterton also provides us with a wholly original and imaginative perspective on the life of Christ, almost certainly the most widely-known and influential narrative in the Western canon. Here, the narrator is neither Jesus nor disciple, saint or apostle. Instead, it's a donkey who recounts his history and his moment of glory: the Biblical event of Palm Sunday, when Jesus rode into Jerusalem on a donkey and a jubilant crowd scattered palm branches in his path.

When fishes flew and forests walked
And figs grew upon thorn,
Some moment when the moon was blood
Then surely I was born.

With monstrous head and sickening cry
And ears like errant wings,
The devil's walking parody
Of all four-footed things.

The tattered outlaw of the earth,
Of ancient crooked will;
Starve, scourge, deride me: I am dumb,
I keep my secret still.

Fools! For I also had my hour,
One far fierce hour and sweet.
There was a shout about my ears,
And palms before my feet.

28 March • I Watched a Blackbird • Thomas Hardy

Easter Sunday can fall on any date between 22 March and 25 April. Here is one Easter Day encounter in poetry, between Thomas Hardy and a blackbird. Hardy was a prolific writer and wrote great works, including the novels *Far from the Madding Crowd*, *Jude the Obscure* and *Tess of the d'Urbervilles*. Hardy himself would probably have been surprised to learn that today he's more renowned for his books than his verse, as he always identified more as a poet.

I watched a blackbird on a budding sycamore
One Easter Day, when sap was stirring twigs to the core;
    I saw his tongue, and crocus-coloured bill
    Parting and closing as he turned his trill;
    Then he flew down, seized on a stem of hay,
And upped to where his building scheme was under way,
As if so sure a nest were never shaped on spray.

28 March • Easter Wings • George Herbert

'Easter Wings' is an example of a shape or pattern poem, and the poem's visual form literally illustrates the wings of the title. Easter commemorates the sacrifice of Jesus on the cross and his rebirth. The poem echoes this progression from sorrow to joy.

Lord, who createdst man in wealth and store,
Though foolishly he lost the same,
Decaying more and more,
Till he became
Most poor:
With thee
O let me rise
As larks, harmoniously,
And sing this day thy victories:
Then shall the fall further the flight in me.

My tender age in sorrow did begin
And still with sicknesses and shame
Thou didst so punish sin,
That I became
Most thin.
With thee
Let me combine,
And feel this day thy victory:
For, if I imp my wing on thine,
Affliction shall advance the flight in me.

29 March • Loveliest of Trees, the Cherry Now • A. E. Housman

It is an Easter tradition to wear white clothing – and in A. E. Housman's poem, it is the cherry trees that are dressed in white, first in blossom, then in snow. The poet thinks of his full 'threescore years and ten', or seventy years, which is the biblical average life span. If life is so short, then we should be enjoying the beautiful moments not just in spring, but in winter too. Like Robert Herrick's poem on daffodils (see 15 March), this is a *carpe diem* poem, a poem that urges us to 'seize the day'.

Loveliest of trees, the cherry now
Is hung with bloom along the bough,
And stands about the woodland ride
Wearing white for Eastertide.

Now, of my threescore years and ten,
Twenty will not come again,
And take from seventy springs a score,
It only leaves me fifty more.

And since to look at things in bloom
Fifty springs are little room,
About the woodlands I will go
To see the cherry hung with snow.

29 March • Easter Day • Oscar Wilde

Oscar Wilde is something of a rebellious voice within poetry. In this sonnet on the occasion of Easter, Wilde describes vividly the overwhelming majesty and splendour of the Pope in Rome. Yet the poet contrasts these regal images with the ancient origins of Christianity, and ends with the simple image of an exhausted Christ wandering alone millennia before.

The silver trumpets rang across the Dome:
  The people knelt upon the ground with awe:
  And borne upon the necks of men I saw,
Like some great God, the Holy Lord of Rome.
Priest-like, he wore a robe more white than foam,
  And, king-like, swathed himself in royal red,
  Three crowns of gold rose high upon his head:
In splendour and in light the Pope passed home.
My heart stole back across wide wastes of years
  To One who wandered by a lonely sea,
  And sought in vain for any place of rest:
'Foxes have holes, and every bird its nest,
I, only I, must wander wearily,
And bruise My feet, and drink wine salt with tears.'

30 March • Bitter State • Duranka Perera

While Easter Sunday is a time for celebration throughout the Christian world, it will forever be associated with tragedy and loss in Sri Lanka, where a series of devastating terrorist attacks were carried out on that date in 2019. This piece by the slam poet and practising doctor Duranka Perera gives a powerful and personal account of the anger, anguish and resilience experienced by the Sri Lankan people in the wake of the bombings. Perera lives in the east of England, and, in this poem, he describes his pain at being a world away from his native country in a time of crisis – a feeling that will doubtless be familiar to many.

I was angry when it happened.

I was angry when the numbers continued to rise.

I was angry when bitter tongues lashed old wounds.

I was angry when a dying monument drew more money than
the dying themselves.

I was angry when my words weren't heard.

I was angry that I was told to watch and wait till the dust had
settled, when all I wanted was to dive right in.

I was angry that I was here, safe, distant, impotent, that the
thought of wanting to do something meant feeding my ego
before the orphaned.

I was angry that three tragedies have crushed my country in
my short lifetime.

I'm so angry that my voice is beginning to choke.

But I won't stop shouting
So long as there is hope.

30 March • The Desired Swan-Song • Samuel Taylor Coleridge

This humorous couplet is based on the ancient belief that, having been silent their entire lives, swans sing a beautiful song in the moment before they die. The term 'swansong' has come to describe a final performance or achievement just before the death of a creative artist.

> Swans sing before they die – 'twere no bad thing
> Should certain persons die before they sing.

31 March • Against Idleness and Mischief • Isaac Watts

In this poem, Isaac Watts is trying to argue that there is a moral purpose to keeping busy.

How doth the little busy bee
  Improve each shining hour,
And gather honey all the day
  From every opening flower!

How skilfully she builds her cell!
  How neat she spreads the wax!
And labours hard to store it well
  With the sweet food she makes.

In works of labour or of skill,
  I would be busy too;
For Satan finds some mischief still
  For idle hands to do.

In books, or work, or healthful play,
  Let my first years be passed,
That I may give for every day
  Some good account at last.

31 March • How Doth the Little Crocodile • Lewis Carroll

A parody is a way of poking fun at something by imitating its style – in this case, Lewis Carroll is parodying the previous didactic work by Isaac Watts. This short poem appears in Carroll's 1865 novel *Alice in Wonderland*: it is recited by Alice in Chapter Two.

How doth the little crocodile
  Improve his shining tail,
And pour the waters of the Nile
  On every golden scale!

How cheerfully he seems to grin,
  How neatly spread his claws,
And welcomes little fishes in
  With gently smiling jaws!

April

1 April • April Fool • Louis MacNeice

Pinch, punch, first of the month! It's April Fool's Day, a time for practical jokes and hoaxes. The Irish poet Louis MacNeice wrote this poem in the early part of the twentieth century. Incidentally, the earliest recorded foolishness on 1 April is a trick played by a fox in Chaucer's *Canterbury Tales*, which dates from the late fourteenth century.

Here come I, old April Fool,
Between March hare and nuts in May.
Fool me forward, fool me back,
Hares will dance and nuts will crack.

Here come I, my fingers crossed
Between the shuffle and the deal.
Fool me flush or fool me straight,
Queens are wild and queens will wait.

Here come I, my clogs worn out
Between the burden and the song.
Fool me hither, fool me hence,
Keep the sound but ditch the sense.

Here come I, my hair on fire,
Between the devil and the deep.
Fool me over, fool me down,
Sea shall dry and devil shall drown.

Here come I, in guts and brass,
Between the raven and the pit.
Fool me under, fool me flat,
Coffins land on Ararat.

Here come I, old April Fool,
Between the hoar frost and the fall.
Fool me drunk or fool me dry,
Spring comes back, and back come I.

1 April • Jabberwocky • Lewis Carroll

It's hard to think of a poem sillier than 'Jabberwocky'. Lewis Carroll included 'Jabberwocky' in his novel *Through the Looking Glass, and What Alice Found There*, the sequel to *Alice in Wonderland*. You might come to the same conclusion as Alice: 'It seems very pretty . . . but it's *rather* hard to understand!' Some of Carroll's nonsense words have since made their way into the dictionary, such as 'chortle', which means laugh.

'Twas brillig, and the slithy toves
  Did gyre and gimble in the wabe:
All mimsy were the borogoves,
  And the mome raths outgrabe.

'Beware the Jabberwock, my son!
  The jaws that bite, the claws that catch!
Beware the Jubjub bird, and shun
  The frumious Bandersnatch!'

He took his vorpal sword in hand;
  Long time the manxome foe he sought—
So rested he by the Tumtum tree
  And stood awhile in thought.

And, as in uffish thought he stood,
  The Jabberwock, with eyes of flame,
Came whiffling through the tulgey wood,
  And burbled as it came!

One, two! One, two! And through and through
    The vorpal blade went snicker-snack!
He left it dead, and with its head
    He went galumphing back.

'And hast thou slain the Jabberwock?
    Come to my arms, my beamish boy!
O frabjous day! Callooh! Callay!'
    He chortled in his joy.

'Twas brillig, and the slithy toves
    Did gyre and gimble in the wabe:
All mimsy were the borogoves,
    And the mome raths outgrabe.

2 April • The Walrus and the Carpenter • Lewis Carroll

April Fool's Day might have been and gone, but there's always time for a little more nonsense. This poem also originally appeared in Lewis Carroll's *Through the Looking Glass*. It is recited to Alice by the characters Tweedledum and Tweedledee. In the novel, Alice concludes that both the Walrus and the Carpenter are 'very unpleasant characters' – and, as it happens, so are Tweedledum and Tweedledee!

The sun was shining on the sea,
  Shining with all his might:
He did his very best to make
  The billows smooth and bright –
And this was odd, because it was
  The middle of the night.

The moon was shining sulkily,
  Because she thought the sun
Had got no business to be there
  After the day was done –
'It's very rude of him,' she said,
  'To come and spoil the fun.'

The sea was wet as wet could be,
  The sands were dry as dry.
You could not see a cloud, because
  No cloud was in the sky:
No birds were flying overhead –
  There were no birds to fly.

The Walrus and the Carpenter
  Were walking close at hand:
They wept like anything to see
  Such quantities of sand:
'If this were only cleared away,'
  They said, 'it *would* be grand!'

'If seven maids with seven mops
  Swept it for half a year,
Do you suppose,' the Walrus said,
  'That they could get it clear?'
'I doubt it,' said the Carpenter,
  And shed a bitter tear.

'O Oysters, come and walk with us!'
  The Walrus did beseech.
'A pleasant walk, a pleasant talk,
  Along the briny beach:
We cannot do with more than four,
  To give a hand to each.'

The eldest Oyster looked at him,
  But never a word he said:
The eldest Oyster winked his eye,
  And shook his heavy head –
Meaning to say he did not choose
  To leave the oyster-bed.

But four young Oysters hurried up,
  All eager for the treat:
Their coats were brushed, their faces washed,
  Their shoes were clean and neat –
And this was odd, because, you know,
  They hadn't any feet.

Four other Oysters followed them,
And yet another four;
And thick and fast they came at last,
And more, and more, and more –
All hopping through the frothy waves,
And scrambling to the shore.

The Walrus and the Carpenter
Walked on a mile or so,
And then they rested on a rock
Conveniently low:
And all the little Oysters stood
And waited in a row.

'The time has come,' the Walrus said,
'To talk of many things:
Of shoes – and ships – and sealing-wax –
Of cabbages – and kings –
And why the sea is boiling hot –
And whether pigs have wings.'

'But wait a bit,' the Oysters cried,
'Before we have our chat:
For some of us are out of breath,
And all of us are fat!'
'No hurry!' said the Carpenter.
They thanked him much for that.

'A loaf of bread,' the Walrus said,
'Is what we chiefly need:
Pepper and vinegar besides
Are very good indeed –
Now if you're ready, Oysters dear,
We can begin to feed.'

'But not on us!' the Oysters cried,
    Turning a little blue.
'After such kindness, that would be
    A dismal thing to do!'
'The night is fine,' the Walrus said.
    'Do you admire the view?

'It was so kind of you to come!
    And you are very nice!'
The Carpenter said nothing but
    'Cut us another slice:
I wish you were not quite so deaf –
    I've had to ask you twice!'

'It seems a shame,' the Walrus said,
    'To play them such a trick.
After we've brought them out so far,
    And made them trot so quick!'
The Carpenter said nothing but
    'The butter's spread too thick!'

'I weep for you,' the Walrus said:
    'I deeply sympathize.'
With sobs and tears he sorted out
    Those of the largest size,
Holding his pocket-handkerchief
    Before his streaming eyes.

'O Oysters,' said the Carpenter,
    'You've had a pleasant run!
Shall we be trotting home again?'
    But answer came there none –
And this was scarcely odd, because
    They'd eaten every one.

2 April • The Mad Gardener's Song • Lewis Carroll

This nonsense poem, with its confusing mixture of animals, people and absolute ridiculousness, is the best-known part of Lewis Carroll's lesser-known novel, *Sylvie and Bruno.*

He thought he saw an Elephant
That practised on a fife:
He looked again, and found it was
A letter from his wife.
'At length I realize,' he said,
'The bitterness of Life!'

He thought he saw a Buffalo
Upon the chimney-piece:
He looked again, and found it was
His Sister's Husband's Niece.
'Unless you leave this house,' he said,
'I'll send for the Police!'

He thought he saw a Rattlesnake
That questioned him in Greek:
He looked again, and found it was
The Middle of Next Week.
'The one thing I regret,' he said,
'Is that it cannot speak!'

He thought he saw a Banker's Clerk
Descending from the 'bus:
He looked again, and found it was
A Hippopotamus.
'If this should stay to dine,' he said,
'There won't be much for us!'

He thought he saw a Kangaroo
That worked a coffee-mill:
He looked again, and found it was
A Vegetable-Pill.
'Were I to swallow this,' he said,
'I should be very ill!'

He thought he saw a Coach-and-Four
That stood beside his bed:
He looked again, and found it was
A Bear without a Head.
'Poor thing,' he said, 'poor silly thing!
It's waiting to be fed!'

He thought he saw an Albatross
That fluttered round the lamp:
He looked again, and found it was
A Penny-Postage-Stamp.
'You'd best be getting home,' he said,
'The nights are very damp!'

He thought he saw a Garden-Door
That opened with a key:
He looked again, and found it was
A Double Rule of Three:
'And all its mystery,' he said,
'Is clear as day to me!'

He thought he saw an Argument
That proved he was the Pope:
He looked again, and found it was
A Bar of Mottled Soap.
'A fact so dread,' he faintly said,
'Extinguishes all hope!'

3 April • The Jumblies • Edward Lear

Lewis Carroll and Edward Lear were the kings of nonsense writing. Lear is best known for the narrative poem 'The Owl and the Pussycat', and he also helped to popularize the limerick form ('There once was a poet named Lear . . .'). 'The Jumblies' is an example of one of Lear's most inventive and madcap poems.

I

They went to sea in a Sieve, they did,
  In a Sieve they went to sea:
In spite of all their friends could say,
On a winter's morn, on a stormy day,
  In a Sieve they went to sea!
And when the Sieve turned round and round,
And every one cried, 'You'll all be drowned!'
They called aloud, 'Our Sieve ain't big,
But we don't care a button! we don't care a fig!
  In a Sieve we'll go to sea!'
    Far and few, far and few,
      Are the lands where the Jumblies live;
    Their heads are green, and their hands are blue,
      And they went to sea in a Sieve.

II

They sailed away in a Sieve, they did,
  In a Sieve they sailed so fast,
With only a beautiful pea-green veil
Tied with a riband by way of a sail,
  To a small tobacco-pipe mast;
And every one said, who saw them go,
'O won't they be soon upset, you know!
For the sky is dark, and the voyage is long,
And happen what may, it's extremely wrong
  In a Sieve to sail so fast!'
    Far and few, far and few,
      Are the lands where the Jumblies live;
    Their heads are green, and their hands are blue,
      And they went to sea in a Sieve.

III

The water it soon came in, it did,
  The water it soon came in;
So to keep them dry, they wrapped their feet
In a pinky paper all folded neat,
  And they fastened it down with a pin.
And they passed the night in a crockery-jar,
And each of them said, 'How wise we are!
Though the sky be dark, and the voyage be long,
Yet we never can think we were rash or wrong,
  While round in our Sieve we spin!'
    Far and few, far and few,
      Are the lands where the Jumblies live;
    Their heads are green, and their hands are blue,
      And they went to sea in a Sieve.

IV

And all night long they sailed away;
  And when the sun went down,
They whistled and warbled a moony song
To the echoing sound of a coppery gong,
  In the shade of the mountains brown.
'O Timballo! How happy we are,
When we live in a sieve and a crockery-jar,
And all night long in the moonlight pale,
We sail away with a pea-green sail,
  In the shade of the mountains brown!'
    Far and few, far and few,
      Are the lands where the Jumblies live;
    Their heads are green, and their hands are blue,
      And they went to sea in a Sieve.

V

They sailed to the Western Sea, they did,
  To a land all covered with trees,
And they bought an Owl, and a useful Cart,
And a pound of Rice, and a Cranberry Tart,
  And a hive of silvery Bees.
And they bought a Pig, and some green Jack-daws,
And a lovely Monkey with lollipop paws,
And forty bottles of Ring-Bo-Ree,
  And no end of Stilton Cheese.
    Far and few, far and few,
      Are the lands where the Jumblies live;
    Their heads are green, and their hands are blue,
      And they went to sea in a Sieve.

VI

And in twenty years they all came back,
  In twenty years or more,
And every one said, 'How tall they've grown!'
For they've been to the Lakes, and the Torrible Zone,
  And the hills of the Chankly Bore;
And they drank their health, and gave them a feast
Of dumplings made of beautiful yeast;
And every one said, 'If we only live,
We too will go to sea in a Sieve, –
  To the hills of the Chankly Bore!'
    Far and few, far and few,
      Are the lands where the Jumblies live;
    Their heads are green, and their hands are blue,
      And they went to sea in a Sieve.

3 April • The Spider and the Fly • Mary Botham Howitt

In this, her most well-known poem, published in 1829, the English writer Mary Botham Howitt entertains us with a cautionary tale . . .

'Will you walk into my parlour?' said the Spider to the Fly,
''Tis the prettiest little parlour that ever you did spy;
The way into my parlour is up a winding stair,
And I've got many curious things to show when you are there.'
'Oh no, no,' said the little Fly, 'to ask me is in vain,
For who goes up your winding stair can ne'er come down again.'

'I'm sure you must be weary, dear, with soaring up so high;
Will you rest upon my little bed?' said the Spider to the Fly.
'There are pretty curtains drawn around; the sheets are fine and thin,
And if you like to rest awhile, I'll snugly tuck you in!'
'Oh no, no,' said the little Fly, 'for I've often heard it said,
They never, never wake again, who sleep upon your bed!'

Said the cunning Spider to the Fly, 'Dear friend what can I do,
To prove the warm affection I've always felt for you?
I have within my pantry good store of all that's nice;
I'm sure you're very welcome – will you please to take a slice?'
'Oh no, no,' said the little Fly, 'kind sir, that cannot be,
I've heard what's in your pantry, and I do not wish to see!'

'Sweet creature!' said the Spider, 'you're witty and you're wise,
How handsome are your gauzy wings, how brilliant are your eyes!
I've a little looking-glass upon my parlour shelf,
If you'll step in one moment, dear, you shall behold yourself.'
'I thank you, gentle sir,' she said, 'for what you're pleased to say,
And bidding you good morning now, I'll call another day.'

The Spider turned him round about, and went into his den,
For well he knew the silly Fly would soon come back again:
So he wove a subtle web, in a little corner sly,
And set his table ready, to dine upon the Fly.
Then he came out to his door again, and merrily did sing,
'Come hither, hither, pretty Fly, with the pearl and silver wing;
Your robes are green and purple – there's a crest upon your head;
Your eyes are like the diamond bright, but mine are dull as lead!'

Alas, alas! how very soon this silly little Fly,
Hearing his wily, flattering words, came slowly flitting by;
With buzzing wings she hung aloft, then near and nearer drew,
Thinking only of her brilliant eyes, and green and purple hue –
Thinking only of her crested head – poor foolish thing! At last,
Up jumped the cunning Spider, and fiercely held her fast.
He dragged her up his winding stair, into his dismal den,
Within his little parlour – but she ne'er came out again!

And now, dear little children, who may this story read,
To idle, silly flattering words, I pray you ne'er give heed:
Unto an evil counsellor, close heart and ear and eye,
And take a lesson from this tale, of the Spider and the Fly.

4 April • The Mock Turtle's Song • Lewis Carroll

In Victorian times, mock turtle soup was a popular dish that used cheap cuts and offal to look like expensive turtle meat. In *Alice in Wonderland*, Alice meets a creature called the Mock Turtle, a pun on the name of this popular soup, as there really was no such creature. 'The Mock Turtle's Song', which he performs for Alice accompanied by a dance, is a parody of the previous poem by Mary Botham Howitt.

'Will you walk a little faster?' said a whiting to a snail.
'There's a porpoise close behind us, and he's treading on my tail.
See how eagerly the lobsters and the turtles all advance!
They are waiting on the shingle— will you come and join the dance?
  Will you, won't you, will you, won't you, will you join the dance?
  Will you, won't you, will you, won't you, won't you join the dance?

'You can really have no notion how delightful it will be
When they take us up and throw us, with the lobsters, out to sea!'
But the snail replied 'Too far, too far!' and gave a look askance—
Said he thanked the whiting kindly, but he would not join the dance.
  Would not, could not, would not, could not, would not join the dance.
  Would not, could not, would not, could not, could not join the dance.

'What matters it how far we go?' his scaly friend replied.
'There is another shore, you know, upon the other side.
The further off from England the nearer is to France—
Then turn not pale, beloved snail, but come and join the dance?
  Will you, won't you, will you, won't you, won't you join the dance?
  Will you, won't you, will you, won't you, won't you join the dance?'

4 **April** • Who Killed Cock Robin? • Anon.

Robert Walpole became Britain's first Prime Minister on this day in 1721. He was in power until 1742 – the longest-serving Prime Minister in British history – but he eventually fell from power after a group of detractors rose against him. It is popularly thought that these lines relate to Walpole's downfall. Despite the bloody theme of the song, which has featured in many novels and murder mysteries, there is a childlike quality to the short lines and neat rhymes.

Who killed Cock Robin?
  'I,' said the Sparrow,
  'With my little bow and arrow,
I killed Cock Robin.'

Who saw him die?
  'I,' said the Fly,
  'With my little eye,
I saw him die.'

Who'll dig his grave?
  'I,' said the Owl,
  'With my spade and show'l,
I'll dig his grave.'

Who'll be the Parson?
  'I,' said the Rook,
  'With my little book,
I'll be the Parson.'

Who will be chief mourner?
  'I,' said the Dove,
  'For I mourn my love,
I shall be chief mourner.'

Who'll sing a psalm?
  'I,' said the Thrush,
  'As I sit in a bush.
I'll sing a psalm.'

Who'll carry the coffin?
  'I,' said the Kite,
  'If it's not in the night,
I'll carry the coffin.'

Who'll toll the bell?
  'I,' said the Bull,
  'Because I can pull,
I'll toll the bell.'

All the birds of the air
  Fell sighing and sobbing,
  When they heard the bell toll
For poor Cock Robin.

5 April • First Word (After Helen Keller) • Rachel Rooney

In 1904, Helen Keller became the first deaf and blind person to graduate from university. Her remarkable story can be traced back to 5 April 1887, when she learned her first words. Her hand was held under the flow water from a pump, and the letters for 'water' were spelt on her other palm. This poem captures the moment that the mystery of language was revealed to her.

This thing she's feeling
is nameless cold
that can't be held.
This unheard sound
its unseen lettering
drums her outstretched skin
like fingertips.
This thing is spilling over.

This thing she's feeling
in her other palm
is nameless warm.
This unseen sound
its unheard lettering
drums her outstretched skin
like drops of rain.
This thing is spelling water.

5 **April** • You Are Old, Father William • Lewis Carroll

This poem, also featured in *Alice in Wonderland*, is a mischievous parody of Robert Southey's poem 'The Old Man's Comforts'. In Southey's poem, Father William explains that the reason he has found such contentment in his old age is because he led a virtuous, restrained life in his youth, and always 'remembered my God'. Carroll literally turns this poem on its head, as his Father William 'incessantly' stands on his head, as well as arguing the benefits of a life full of pleasure, arguments, extreme physical activity and magical ointment.

'You are old, Father William,' the young man said,
'And your hair has become very white;
And yet you incessantly stand on your head –
Do you think, at your age, it is right?'

'In my youth,' Father William replied to his son,
'I feared it might injure the brain;
But, now that I'm perfectly sure I have none,
Why, I do it again and again.'

'You are old,' said the youth, 'as I mentioned before,
And have grown most uncommonly fat;
Yet you turned a back-somersault in at the door –
Pray, what is the reason of that?'

‘In my youth,’ said the sage, as he shook his grey locks,
  ‘I kept all my limbs very supple
By the use of this ointment – one shilling the box –
  Allow me to sell you a couple?’

‘You are old,’ said the youth, ‘and your jaws are too weak
  For anything tougher than suet;
Yet you finished the goose, with the bones and the beak –
  Pray, how did you manage to do it?’

‘In my youth,’ said his father, ‘I took to the law,
  And argued each case with my wife;
And the muscular strength, which it gave to my jaw,
  Has lasted the rest of my life.’

‘You are old,’ said the youth, ‘one would hardly suppose
  That your eye was as steady as ever;
Yet you balanced an eel on the end of your nose –
  What made you so awfully clever?’

‘I have answered three questions, and that is enough,’
  Said his father. ‘Don’t give yourself airs!
Do you think I can listen all day to such stuff?
  Be off, or I’ll kick you downstairs!’

6 April • The People of the Eastern Ice • Rudyard Kipling

On 6 April 1909, the American explorer Robert Peary reported that he had become the first man to reach the North Pole. Though Rudyard Kipling never visited the Arctic, he nevertheless wrote this poem as an introduction to the *Jungle Book* story 'Quiquern'. 'Quiquern' is a monstrous dog spirit in Inuit mythology, and Kipling's tale follows two Inuit men as they hunt for food for their starving tribe. Today, the poem has new relevance, as a song of an endangered culture 'melting like snow' takes on fresh meaning in the age of climate change.

The People of the Eastern Ice, they are melting like the snow –
They beg for coffee and sugar; they go where the white men go.
The People of the Western Ice, they learn to steal and fight;
They sell their furs to the trading-post; they sell their souls to the white.
The People of the Southern Ice, they trade with the whaler's crew;
Their women have many ribbons, but their tents are torn and few.
But the People of the Elder Ice, beyond the white man's ken –
Their spears are made of the narwhal-horn, and they are the last of the Men!

6 April • Old Mother Hubbard • Anon.

This popular nursery rhyme was first printed in 1805, although it is thought to date from possibly even centuries before. There is one theory that the poem was written in Tudor times as a mockery of Cardinal Wolsey's failed attempt to obtain an annulment of Henry VIII's marriage to Katherine of Aragon. So 'Mother Hubbard' is Wolsey, the 'bone' is the divorce agreement he was seeking to get for the 'doggie' – the king!

Old Mother Hubbard
Went to the cupboard,
To give the poor dog a bone;
When she came there,
The cupboard was bare,
And so the poor dog got none.

She went to the baker's
To buy him some bread;
But when she got back
The poor dog was dead.

She went to the joiner's
To buy him a coffin;
But when she got back
The doggie was laughing.

She took a clean dish
To get him some tripe;
But when she came back
He was smoking his pipe.

She went to the fishmonger's
To buy him some fish;
And when she came back
He was licking the dish.

She went to the tavern
For white wine and red;
But when she came back
The dog stood on his head.

She went to the hatter's
To buy him a hat;
But when she came back
He was feeding the cat.

She went to the cobbler's
To buy him some shoes;
But when she came back
He was reading the news.

The Dame made a curtsy,
The dog made a bow;
The Dame said, 'Your servant,'
The dog said, 'Bow-wow.'

This wonderful dog
Was Dame Hubbard's delight;
He could sing, he could dance,
He could read, he could write.

She gave him rich dainties
Whenever he fed,
And erected a monument
When he was dead.

7 April • *from* The Prologue to the Canterbury Tales • Geoffrey Chaucer

These are the opening lines to one of the greatest works in English literature, Chaucer's *Canterbury Tales*. Written in Middle English, it is sometimes easier to make sense of the language when speaking it aloud. The narrator speaks of the day in April when he first joins pilgrims at a Southwark pub to set out on the road to Canterbury.

Whan that Aprille with his shoures soote,
The droghte of March hath perced to the roote,
And bathed every veyne in swich licóur
Of which vertú engendred is the flour;
Whan Zephirus eek with his swete breeth
Inspired hath in every holt and heeth
The tendre croppes, and the yonge sonne
Hath in the Ram his halfe cours y-ronne,
And smale fowles maken melodye,
That slepen al the nyght with open ye,
(So priketh hem Natúre in hir corages),
Thanne longen folk to goon on pilgrimages,
And palmeres for to seken straunge strondes,
To ferne halwes, kowthe in sondry londes;
And specially, from every shires ende
Of Engelond, to Caunterbury they wende,
The hooly blisful martir for to seke,
That hem hath holpen whan that they were seeke.
Bifil that in that seson on a day,
In Southwerk at the Tabard as I lay
Redy to wenden on my pilgrymage

To Caunterbury with ful devout corage,
At nyght were come into that hostelrye
Wel nyne and twenty in a compaignye
Of sondry folk, by áventure y-falle
In felaweshipe, and pilgrimes were they alle,
That toward Caunterbury wolden ryde.
The chambres and the stables weren wyde,
And wel we weren esed atte beste.
And shortly, whan the sonne was to reste,
So hadde I spoken with hem everichon,
That I was of hir felaweshipe anon,
And made forward erly for to ryse,
To take oure wey, ther as I yow devyse.

7 April • Mrs Darwin • Carol Ann Duffy

In 1859, Charles Darwin published his groundbreaking theory of evolution, *The Origin of the Species*, which argues that the human race shares a common ancestor with other primates such as gorillas, chimpanzees, monkeys and bonobos. In dating this comic poem 7 April 1852, Carol Ann Duffy is making the suggestion that the idea may have come from Mrs Darwin.

7 April 1852.

Went to the Zoo.
I said to Him –
Something about that Chimpanzee over there
    reminds me
      of you.

8 April • Home-Thoughts from Abroad • Robert Browning

Browning wrote this poem during his 1845 travels around Italy. This is a poem of nostalgia in its truest sense – it comes from the Greek word 'nostos', which means home-coming. Browning might be on holiday, but all he can think of is the beauty of England in springtime, where birds are chirping, flowers blossoming, and nature is coming back to life.

Oh, to be in England
Now that April's there,
And whoever wakes in England
Sees, some morning, unaware,
That the lowest boughs and the brushwood sheaf
Round the elm-tree bole are in tiny leaf,
While the chaffinch sings on the orchard bough
In England – now!

And after April, when May follows,
And the whitethroat builds, and all the swallows!
Hark, where my blossomed pear-tree in the hedge
Leans to the field and scatters on the clover
Blossoms and dewdrops – at the bent spray's edge –
That's the wise thrush; he sings each song twice over,
Lest you should think he never could recapture
The first fine careless rapture!
And though the fields look rough with hoary dew,
All will be gay when noontide wakes anew
The buttercups, the little children's dower
– Far brighter than this gaudy melon-flower!

8 April • Awakening • Tony Mitton

The poet himself has written this illuminating paragraph about his poem:

'The story has been passed down that the Buddha (Siddhartha Gautama) achieved a sudden and powerful experience of understanding after many years of study and practice. Exhausted by the efforts he had made to get to grips with the meaning of his life, he gave up and sat down in meditation under the Bodhi tree, vowing not to get up until some answer presented itself to him. After sitting all night in meditation he caught sight of the morning star rising. The clarity and power of the moment that followed is sometimes called his Enlightenment (or Awakening). In spite of his already great learning and wisdom, all he could say in response to the experience was, "What is this?"'

The Buddha sat silently
under a tree.
He sat and he waited
determinedly.

He sat like a statue
and scarcely stirred.
Out of his lips
came never a word.

He sat through the hours
of an Orient night,
and, just at the edges
of opening light,

up in the heaven,
so sharp and so far,
glimmered the spark
of a wakening star.

Sitting in stillness,
the sight that he saw
pierced him through
to the innermost core.

And all he could say
in his moment of bliss
was simply and purely,
'What is this?'

9 April • The Ballad of Semmerwater • William Watson

Semmerwater, more usually spelt 'Semerwater', is one of the largest lakes in Yorkshire, and a home to many great poets over the centuries. Sir William Watson was one such poet, and he uses Semerwater as the basis for a story about poverty, charity and selfishness. The moral of the story is that even the proudest of empires will fall if it earns the curse of its poor and vulnerable.

Deep asleep, deep asleep,
Deep asleep it lies,
The still lake of Semmerwater,
Under the still skies.

And many a fathom, many a fathom,
Many a fathom below,
In a king's tower and a queen's bower
The fishes come and go.

Once there stood by Semmerwater
A mickle town and tall;
King's tower and queen's bower,
And the wakeman on the wall.

Came a beggar halt and sore:
'I faint for lack of bread.'
King's tower and queen's bower
Cast him forth unfed.

He knocked at the door of the herdsman's cot,
The herdsman's cot in the dale.
They gave him of their oat-cake,
They gave him of their ale.

He cursed aloud that city proud,
He cursed it in its pride;
He cursed it into Semmerwater
Down the brant hillside;
He cursed it into Semmerwater,
There to bide.

King's tower and queen's bower,
And a mickle town and tall;
By glimmer of scale and gleam of fin,
Folk have seen them all.

King's tower and queen's bower,
And weed and reed in the gloom,
And a lost city in Semmerwater
Deep asleep till Doom.

9 April • Wynken, Blynken and Nod • Eugene Field

In this poem, which is another example of nonsense verse, Eugene Field creates a fantastical bedtime story.

Wynken, Blynken, and Nod one night
 Sailed off in a wooden shoe,—
Sailed on a river of crystal light
 Into a sea of dew.
'Where are you going, and what do you wish?'
 The old moon asked the three.
'We have come to fish for the herring-fish
 That live in this beautiful sea;
 Nets of silver and gold have we,'
  Said Wynken,
  Blynken,
  And Nod.

The old moon laughed and sang a song,
 As they rocked in the wooden shoe;
And the wind that sped them all night long
 Ruffled the waves of dew;
The little stars were the herring-fish
 That lived in the beautiful sea.
'Now cast your nets wherever you wish,—
 Never afraid are we!'
 So cried the stars to the fishermen three,
  Wynken,
  Blynken,
  And Nod.

All night long their nets they threw
  To the stars in the twinkling foam,—
Then down from the skies came the wooden shoe,
  Bringing the fishermen home:
'Twas all so pretty a sail, it seemed
  As if it could not be;
And some folk thought 'twas a dream they'd dreamed
  Of sailing that beautiful sea;
  But I shall name you the fishermen three:
        Wynken,
        Blynken,
        And Nod.

Wynken and Blynken are two little eyes,
  And Nod is a little head,
And the wooden shoe that sailed the skies
  Is a wee one's trundle-bed;
So shut your eyes while Mother sings
  Of wonderful sights that be,
And you shall see the beautiful things
  As you rock in the misty sea
  Where the old shoe rocked the fishermen three:—
        Wynken,
        Blynken,
        And Nod.

10 April • The Sugar-Plum Tree • Eugene Field

This next poem by Eugene Field describes a scene just as unusual as Wynken, Blynken and Nod's fishing excursion! Not only is the fruit of this sugar-plum tree 'wondrously sweet', but even the animals that live in it sound delicious: a chocolate cat and a gingerbread dog.

Have you ever heard of the Sugar-Plum Tree?
'Tis a marvel of great renown!
It blooms on the shore of the Lollypop sea
In the garden of Shut-Eye Town;
The fruit that it bears is so wondrously sweet
(As those who have tasted it say)
That good little children have only to eat
Of that fruit to be happy next day.

When you've got to the tree, you would have a hard time
To capture the fruit which I sing;
The tree is so tall that no person could climb
To the boughs where the sugar-plums swing!
But up in that tree sits a chocolate cat,
And a gingerbread dog prowls below –
And this is the way you contrive to get at
Those sugar-plums tempting you so:

You say but the word to that gingerbread dog
And he barks with such terrible zest
That the chocolate cat is at once all agog,
As her swelling proportions attest.
And the chocolate cat goes cavorting around
From this leafy limb unto that,
And the sugar-plums tumble, of course, to the
ground –
Hurrah for that chocolate cat!

There are marshmallows, gumdrops, and peppermint
canes,
With stripings of scarlet or gold,
And you carry away of the treasure that rains,
As much as your apron can hold!
So come, little child, cuddle closer to me
In your dainty white nightcap and gown,
And I'll rock you away to that Sugar-Plum Tree
In the garden of Shut-Eye Town.

10 April • Do Not Stand at My Grave and Weep • Mary Elizabeth Frye

Today is the anniversary of the Good Friday Agreement of 1998 – a key moment in the Northern Ireland peace process. This poem, by Mary Elizabeth Frye, became popular in Great Britain after it was read on BBC Radio by the father of a soldier killed during the Troubles in Northern Ireland. Frye first wrote it on a paper shopping bag, and people quickly began to pass the poem around – and, as it grew in fame, many people tried to claim that they had composed it! Nearly seventy years passed before Frye was recognized as its true author.

Do not stand at my grave and weep.
I am not there I do not sleep.

I am a thousand winds that blow.
I am the diamond glints on snow.
I am the sun on ripened grain.
I am the gentle autumn's rain.

When you awaken in the morning's hush,
I am the swift uplifting rush
Of quiet birds in circling flight.
I am the stars that shine at night.

Do not stand at my grave and cry,
I am not there, I did not die.

11 April • In Time of 'The Breaking of Nations' • Thomas Hardy

Hardy wrote this poem in 1915, around a year into the First World War. The setting is a typical rural scene: a farmer toils in a field, and a young couple walks past him. The poem seems to say that these aspects of life – love and simple labour – are timeless, and will outlive war. Incidentally, the title echoes the line from the Book of Jeremiah in the Bible, 'Thou art my battle axe and weapons of war: for with thee will I break in pieces the nations, and with thee will I destroy kingdoms.'

I

Only a man harrowing clods
  In a slow silent walk
With an old horse that stumbles and nods
  Half asleep as they stalk.

II

Only thin smoke without flame
  From the heaps of couch-grass;
Yet this will go onward the same
  Though Dynasties pass.

III

Yonder a maid and her wight
  Come whispering by:
War's annals will cloud into night
  Ere their story die.

11 April • The Tickle Rhyme • Ian Serraillier

Walls and caterpillars don't usually speak, but in this rhyme by Ian Serraillier the personification is necessary: without their conversation, the mystery of who it was that was tickling the wall's back may never have been answered!

'Who's that tickling my back?' said the wall.
'Me,' said a small
Caterpillar.
'I'm learning
To crawl.'

12 April • Dear Yuri • Brian Moses

On 12 April 1961, the Russian cosmonaut Yuri Gagarin became the first human to travel into space. During the same flight, he was also the first person to orbit earth; when his craft, *Vostok 1*, was launched, he shouted out 'Poyekhali!' – Russian for 'Let's go!'

Dear Yuri, I remember you,
the man with the funny name
who the Russians sent into space,
were you desperate for fame?

There surely must have been safer ways
to get into the history books,
perhaps you couldn't rock like Elvis
or you hadn't got James Dean's looks.

Perhaps you couldn't fight like Ali
or make a political speech
so they packed you into a spaceship
and sent you out of Earth's reach.

And Yuri, what was it like
to be way out there in space,
the first to break free of Earth's gravity
and look down on the human race?

Dear Yuri, I wanted to say
that I remember your flight,
I remember your name, Gagarin,
and the newsreel pictures that night.

And you must have pep talked others
when they took off into the blue.
I've forgotten their names, but Yuri,
I'll always remember you.

12 April • Song in Space • Adrian Mitchell

Gagarin spent 108 minutes in space before descending back into the atmosphere and parachuting to safety from his capsule. Gagarin said of his experience that he 'could have gone flying through space forever'. This poem about space travel by Adrian Mitchell imagines a conversation between the first man in space and the Earth below.

When man first flew beyond the sky
He looked back into the world's blue eye.
Man said: What makes your eye so blue?
Earth said: The tears in the ocean do.
Why are the seas so full of tears?
Because I've wept so many thousand years.
Why do you weep as you dance through space?
Because I am the mother of the human race.

13 April • The Song of Wandering Aengus • W. B. Yeats

Many of Yeats's poems draw on ancient mythology and Irish tradition. Here he writes about Aengus, a god of love and youth – but for Yeats he becomes an old figure, pursuing his past.

I went out to the hazel wood,
Because a fire was in my head,
And cut and peeled a hazel wand,
And hooked a berry to a thread;
And when white moths were on the wing,
And moth-like stars were flickering out,
I dropped the berry in a stream
And caught a little silver trout.

When I had laid it on the floor
I went to blow the fire aflame,
But something rustled on the floor,
And someone called me by my name;
It had become a glimmering girl
With apple blossom in her hair
Who called me by my name and ran
And faded through the brightening air.

Though I am old with wandering
Through hollow lands and hilly lands,
I will find out where she has gone,
And kiss her lips and take her hands;
And walk among long dappled grass,
And pluck till time and times are done,
The silver apples of the moon,
The golden apples of the sun.

13 April • Baisakhi • Anon.

Taking place on 13 or 14 April, Baisakhi is the festival of Sikh New Year, which commemorates the founding of the Sikh community in 1699 in an event known as the Khalsa. It is regarded as the most important festival for Sikhs, though it is celebrated as a harvest festival by people of other faiths in the Punjab region.

Crystals of sugar
  swirl
as the sword
  stirs Amrit.

Listening to the tale
of the Five Beloved Ones,

who dodged death
by giving their lives
to God.

14 April • The Woods and Banks • W. H. Davies

Mid-April marks the arrival of cuckoos. They are said to arrive on St. Tiburtius's Day, which is today: Cuckoo Day. W. H. Davies celebrates the unique call that gives the cuckoo its name: cuckoo, cuckoo!

The woods and banks of England now,
  Late coppered with dead leaves and old,
Have made the early violets grow,
  And bulge with knots of primrose gold.
Hear how the blackbird flutes away,
  Whose music scorns to sleep at night:
Hear how the cuckoo shouts all day
  For echoes – to the world's delight:
Hullo, you imp of wonder, you –
  Where are you now, cuckoo? Cuckoo?

14 April • O Captain! My Captain! • Walt Whitman

This poem was written in 1865 by Walt Whitman in response to the assassination of the American president Abraham Lincoln. Lincoln was shot on 14 April 1865, by John Wilkes Booth, an actor. He died the next morning. It is an 'elegy', a poem of mourning for the dead, and the entire piece is an extended metaphor, imagining America as a ship, and Lincoln as the ship's captain.

O Captain! my Captain! our fearful trip is done,
The ship has weather'd every rack, the prize we sought is won,
The port is near, the bells I hear, the people all exulting,
While follow eyes the steady keel, the vessel grim and daring;
But O heart! heart! heart!
O the bleeding drops of red,
Where on the deck my Captain lies,
Fallen cold and dead.

O Captain! my Captain! rise up and hear the bells;
Rise up—for you the flag is flung—for you the bugle trills,
For you bouquets and ribbon'd wreaths—for you the shores a-crowding,
For you they call, the swaying mass, their eager faces turning;
Here Captain! dear father!
This arm beneath your head!
It is some dream that on the deck,
You've fallen cold and dead.

My Captain does not answer, his lips are pale and still,
My father does not feel my arm, he has no pulse nor will,
The ship is anchor'd safe and sound, its voyage closed and
    done,
From fearful trip the victor ship comes in with object won;
                Exult O shores, and ring O bells!
                    But I with mournful tread,
                        Walk the deck my Captain lies,
                            Fallen cold and dead.

15 April • Ode on the Loss of the *Titanic* • Geoffrey Hill

Early on the morning of 15 April 1912, RMS *Titanic* collided with an iceberg and sank in the icy waters of the north Atlantic. Over 1,500 people died – almost three-quarters of the passengers and crew on board. It is fixed in the popular imagination as one of the worst, most shocking maritime disasters of all time. Geoffrey Hill's short lines on the *Titanic* themselves swirl and swell like an angry ocean.

Thriving against façades the ignorant sea
Souses our public baths, statues, waste ground:
Archaic earth-shaker, fresh enemy
('The tables of exchange being overturned');

Drowns Babel in upheaval and display;
Unswerving, as were the admired multitudes
Silenced from time to time under its sway.
By all means let us appease the terse gods.

15 April • The Convergence of the Twain • Thomas Hardy

The RMS *Titanic* was lavishly furnished, creating the 'waste of riches' Hardy refers to when it sank. The poem concentrates on the 'Twain' of the title – the ship and the iceberg – and how they came to collide (or 'converge').

I

In a solitude of the sea
Deep from human vanity,
And the Pride of Life that planned her, stilly couches she.

II

Steel chambers, late the pyres
Of her salamandrine fires,
Cold currents thrid, and turn to rhythmic tidal lyres.

III

Over the mirrors meant
To glass the opulent
The sea-worm crawls – grotesque, slimed, dumb,
indifferent.

IV

Jewels in joy designed
To ravish the sensuous mind
Lie lightless, all their sparkles bleared and black and blind.

V

Dim moon-eyed fishes near
Gaze at the gilded gear
And query: 'What does this vaingloriousness down here?' . . .

VI

Well: while was fashioning
This creature of cleaving wing,
The Immanent Will that stirs and urges everything

VII

Prepared a sinister mate
For her – so gaily great –
A Shape of Ice, for the time far and dissociate.

VIII

And as the smart ship grew
In stature, grace, and hue,
In shadowy silent distance grew the Iceberg too.

IX

Alien they seemed to be:
No mortal eye could see
The intimate welding of their later history,

X

Or sign that they were bent
By paths coincident
On being anon twin halves of one august event,

XI

Till the Spinner of the Years
Said 'Now!' And each one hears,
And consummation comes, and jars two hemispheres.

16 April • Will Ye No Come Back Again? • Carolina Oliphant, Lady Nairne

The Battle of Culloden was fought on 16 April 1746, between a British Loyalist army under the command of the Duke of Cumberland and a Scottish Jacobite force under the command of Charles Edward Stuart ('Bonnie Prince Charlie'). Stuart was the 'Young Pretender' to the British crown, which had been seized from his grandfather King James II in the Glorious Revolution of 1688. This battle – the last one fought on British soil – ended Stuart's efforts to take up the throne of Great Britain and forced him to flee Scotland, never to return. This poem laments his failed attempt and calls for his return to Scotland.

Will ye no come back again?
Will ye no come back again?
Better lo'ed ye canne be,
Will ye no come back again?

Bonnie Charlie's now awa,
    Safely owre the friendly main;
Mony a heart will break in twa,
    Should he ne'er come back again.

Ye trusted in your Hieland men,
    They trusted you, dear Charlie;
They kent you hiding in the glen,
    Your cleadin' was but barely.

English bribes were a' in vain;
An' e'en tho' puirer we may be,
Siller canna buy the heart
That beats aye for thine and thee.

We watched thee in the gloaming hour,
We watched thee in the morning grey;
Tho' thirty thousand pounds they'd gie,
Oh there is nane that wad betray.

Sweet's the laverock's note and lang,
Lilting wildly up the glen;
But aye to me he sings ae sang,–
Will ye no come back again?

Will ye no come back again?
Will ye no come back again?
Better lo'ed ye canne be,
Will ye no come back again?

16 April • The Skye Boat Song • Sir Harold Boulton

Written in the late nineteenth century and set to music many times since, 'The Skye Boat Song' paints a romantic image of Bonnie Prince Charlie's flight to the island of Skye after his army's defeat at Culloden. Although vanquished that day, the poem ends on a rousing patriotic note – one far more assured than the rhetorical question which concludes the previous entry.

Speed, bonnie boat, like a bird on the wing
   Onward, the sailors cry!
Carry the lad that's born to be King
   Over the sea to Skye.

Loud the winds cry, loud the waves roar,
   Thunderclaps rend the air.
Baffled our foes stand by the shore.
   Follow they will not dare

Many's the lad fought on that day
   Well the claymore could wield,
When the night came silently lay
   Dead on Culloden's field.

Burned are our homes, exile and death
   Scatter the loyal men.
Yet ere the sword cool in the sheath
   Scotland will rise again!

17 April • *from* The Waste Land • T. S. Eliot

T. S. Eliot remains one of the most important English poets in history. Much of his poetry filled with unusual words, complex references and even foreign languages! He received the Nobel Prize in Literature in 1948. His great poem *The Waste Land* has many famous lines – not least its opening characterization of the month of April, as well as the enigmatic line: 'I will show you fear in a handful of dust'.

I. The Burial of the Dead

April is the cruellest month, breeding
Lilacs out of the dead land, mixing
Memory and desire, stirring
Dull roots with spring rain.
Winter kept us warm, covering
Earth in forgetful snow, feeding
A little life with dried tubers.
Summer surprised us, coming over the Starnbergersee
With a shower of rain; we stopped in the colonnade,
And went on in sunlight, into the Hofgarten,
And drank coffee, and talked for an hour.
Bin gar keine Russin, stamm' aus Litauen, echt deutsch.
And when we were children, staying at the arch-duke's,
My cousin's, he took me out on a sled,
And I was frightened. He said, Marie,
Marie, hold on tight. And down we went.
In the mountains, there you feel free.
I read, much of the night, and go south in the winter.

What are the roots that clutch, what branches grow
Out of this stony rubbish? Son of man,
You cannot say, or guess, for you know only
A heap of broken images, where the sun beats,
And the dead tree gives no shelter, the cricket no relief,
And the dry stone no sound of water. Only
There is shadow under this red rock,
(Come in under the shadow of this red rock),
And I will show you something different from either
Your shadow at morning striding behind you
Or your shadow at evening rising to meet you;
I will show you fear in a handful of dust.

Frisch weht der Wind
Der Heimat zu,
Mein Irisch Kind,
Wo weilest du?

'You gave me hyacinths first a year ago;
'They called me the hyacinth girl.'
– Yet when we came back, late, from the hyacinth garden,
Your arms full, and your hair wet, I could not
Speak, and my eyes failed, I was neither
Living nor dead, and I knew nothing,
Looking into the heart of light, the silence.

Oed' und leer das Meer.

17 April • Waste Land Limericks • Wendy Cope

Eliot's 'The Waste Land' has inspired many works of literature since it was published, but perhaps none as directly as this by Wendy Cope. Using the humorous form of the five-line limerick, Cope condenses Eliot's famously long and complex masterpiece into five witty stanzas.

I

In April one seldom feels cheerful;
Dry stones, sun and dust make me fearful;
Clairvoyantes distress me,
Commuters depress me –
Met Stetson and gave him an earful.

II

She sat on a mighty fine chair,
Sparks flew as she tidied her hair;
She asks many questions,
I make few suggestions –
Bad as Albert and Lil – what a pair!

III

The Thames runs, bones rattle, rats creep;
Tiresias fancies a peep –
A typist is laid,
A record is played –
Wei la la. After this it gets deep.

IV

A Phoenician named Phlebas forgot
About birds and his business – the lot,
Which is no surprise,
Since he'd met his demise
And been left in the ocean to rot.

V

No water. Dry rocks and dry throats,
Then thunder, a shower of quotes
From the Sanskrit and Dante.
Da. Damyata. Shantih.
I hope you'll make sense of the notes.

18 April • I Wandered Lonely as a Cloud • William Wordsworth

This poem opens with a multitude of natural images: clouds, vales, hills and – most famously – daffodils. While Wordsworth writes at length on the sight of the daffodils, he never mentions their smell. This is unsurprising, as Wordsworth actually suffered from anosmia and had barely any sense of smell at all!

I wandered lonely as a cloud
That floats on high o'er vales and hills,
When all at once I saw a crowd,
A host, of golden daffodils;
Beside the lake, beneath the trees,
Fluttering and dancing in the breeze.

Continuous as the stars that shine
And twinkle on the milky way,
They stretched in never-ending line
Along the margin of a bay:
Ten thousand saw I at a glance,
Tossing their heads in sprightly dance.

The waves beside them danced; but they
Out-did the sparkling waves in glee:
A poet could not but be gay,
In such a jocund company:
I gazed—and gazed—but little thought
What wealth the show to me had brought:

For oft, when on my couch I lie
In vacant or in pensive mood,
They flash upon that inward eye
Which is the bliss of solitude;
And then my heart with pleasure fills,
And dances with the daffodils.

18 April • Paul Revere's Ride • Henry Wadsworth Longfellow

On the eve of the American Revolutionary War (or what we Brits call the American War of Independence), 18 April 1775, Paul Revere rode from Boston to Lexington to warn rebel leaders that British soldiers were on the march and planning to arrest them. His dramatic ride is immortalized here by the American poet, Henry Longfellow.

Listen, my children, and you shall hear
Of the midnight ride of Paul Revere,
On the eighteenth of April, in Seventy-five;
Hardly a man is now alive
Who remembers that famous day and year.

He said to his friend, 'If the British march
By land or sea from the town to-night,
Hang a lantern aloft in the belfry arch
Of the North Church tower as a signal light,—
One, if by land, and two, if by sea;
And I on the opposite shore will be,
Ready to ride and spread the alarm
Through every Middlesex village and farm,
For the country folk to be up and to arm.'

Then he said, 'Good night!' and with muffled oar
Silently rowed to the Charlestown shore,
Just as the moon rose over the bay,
Where swinging wide at her moorings lay
The *Somerset*, British man-of-war;

A phantom ship, with each mast and spar
Across the moon like a prison bar,
And a huge black hulk, that was magnified
By its own reflection in the tide.

Meanwhile, his friend, through alley and street,
Wanders and watches with eager ears,
Till in the silence around him he hears
The muster of men at the barrack door,
The sound of arms, and the tramp of feet,
And the measured tread of the grenadiers,
Marching down to their boats on the shore.

Then he climbed the tower of the old North Church,
By the wooden stairs, with stealthy tread,
To the belfry-chamber overhead,
And startled the pigeons from their perch
On the sombre rafters, that round him made
Masses and moving shapes of shade, –
By the trembling ladder, steep and tall,
To the highest window in the wall,
Where he paused to listen and look down
A moment on the roofs of the town,
And the moonlight flowing over all.

Beneath, in the churchyard, lay the dead,
In their night encampment on the hill,
Wrapped in silence so deep and still
That he could hear, like a sentinel's tread,
The watchful night-wind, as it went
Creeping along from tent to tent,
And seeming to whisper, 'All is well!'
A moment only he feels the spell
Of the place and the hour, and the secret dread

Of the lonely belfry and the dead;
For suddenly all his thoughts are bent
On a shadowy something far away,
Where the river widens to meet the bay, –
A line of black that bends and floats
On the rising tide, like a bridge of boats.

Meanwhile, impatient to mount and ride,
Booted and spurred, with a heavy stride
On the opposite shore walked Paul Revere.
Now he patted his horse's side,
Now gazed at the landscape far and near,
Then, impetuous, stamped the earth,
And turned and tightened his saddle-girth;
But mostly he watched with eager search
The belfry-tower of the old North Church,
As it rose above the graves on the hill,
Lonely and spectral and sombre and still.
And lo! as he looks, on the belfry's height
A glimmer, and then a gleam of light!
He springs to the saddle, the bridle he turns,
But lingers and gazes, till full on his sight
A second lamp in the belfry burns!

A hurry of hoofs in a village street,
A shape in the moonlight, a bulk in the dark,
And beneath, from the pebbles, in passing, a spark
Struck out by a steed flying fearless and fleet:
That was all! And yet, through the gloom and the light,
The fate of a nation was riding that night;
And the spark struck out by that steed, in his flight,
Kindled the land into flame with its heat.

He has left the village and mounted the steep,
And beneath him, tranquil and broad and deep,
Is the Mystic, meeting the ocean tides;
And under the alders, that skirt its edge,
Now soft on the sand, now loud on the ledge,
Is heard the tramp of his steed as he rides.

It was twelve by the village clock,
When he crossed the bridge into Medford town.
He heard the crowing of the cock,
And the barking of the farmer's dog,
And felt the damp of the river fog,
That rises after the sun goes down.

It was one by the village clock,
When he galloped into Lexington.
He saw the gilded weathercock
Swim in the moonlight as he passed,
And the meeting-house windows, blank and bare,
Gaze at him with a spectral glare,
As if they already stood aghast
At the bloody work they would look upon.

It was two by the village clock,
When he came to the bridge in Concord town.
He heard the bleating of the flock,
And the twitter of birds among the trees,
And felt the breath of the morning breeze
Blowing over the meadows brown.
And one was safe and asleep in his bed
Who at the bridge would be first to fall,
Who that day would be lying dead,
Pierced by a British musket-ball.

You know the rest. In the books you have read,
How the British Regulars fired and fled, –
How the farmers gave them ball for ball,
From behind each fence and farm-yard wall,
Chasing the red-coats down the lane,
Then crossing the fields to emerge again
Under the trees at the turn of the road,
And only pausing to fire and load.

So through the night rode Paul Revere;
And so through the night went his cry of alarm
To every Middlesex village and farm, –
A cry of defiance and not of fear,
A voice in the darkness, a knock at the door,
And a word that shall echo for evermore!
For, borne on the night-wind of the Past,
Through all our history, to the last,
In the hour of darkness and peril and need,
The people will waken and listen to hear
The hurrying hoof-beats of that steed,
And the midnight message of Paul Revere.

19 April • Concord Hymn • Ralph Waldo Emerson

On 19 April 1775, the day after Paul Revere's famous midnight ride, the American Revolutionary War had begun. The opening battles took place in Lexington and Concord, Massachusetts. The American philosopher-poet Ralph Waldo Emerson wrote this poem in 1837 for the completion of the battle monument in Concord, the town where he lived.

By the rude bridge that arched the flood,
  Their flag to April's breeze unfurled,
Here once the embattled farmers stood
  And fired the shot heard round the world.

The foe long since in silence slept;
  Alike the conqueror silent sleeps;
And Time the ruined bridge has swept
  Down the dark stream which seaward creeps.

On this green bank, by this soft stream,
  We set today a votive stone;
That memory may their deed redeem,
  When, like our sires, our sons are gone.

Spirit, that made those heroes dare
  To die, and leave their children free,
Bid Time and Nature gently spare
  The shaft we raise to them and thee.

19 April • Be Like the Bird • Victor Hugo

The great French novelist and poet Victor Hugo was born in France in 1802 and is perhaps best known as the author of *The Hunchback of Notre Dame* and *Les Misérables*.

Be like the bird, who
Resting in his flight
On a twig too slight
Feels it bend beneath him
Yet sings,
Knowing he has wings.

20 April • I Had a Dove • John Keats

It is extraordinary to think that John Keats, remembered for writing some of the most beautiful poetry in history, died when he was only twenty-five years old. These lines, on a wild bird kept as a pet that dies in its captivity, reflect upon death in a way that feels especially poignant.

I had a dove, and the sweet dove died;
  And I have thought it died of grieving:
O, what could it grieve for? Its feet were tied,
  With a silken thread of my own hand's weaving;
Sweet little red feet, why should you die?
Why should you leave me, sweet bird, why?
You liv'd alone on the forest tree,
Why, pretty thing! could you not live with me?
I kiss'd you oft and gave you white peas;
Why not live sweetly, as in the green trees?

20 April • Cynddylan on a Tractor • R. S. Thomas

In this poem, R. S. Thomas uses the description of the farmer Cynddylan's first ride on his brand-new tractor to explore some of the concerns he has about industrialization coming to the farms of his native Wales.

Ah, you should see Cynddylan on a tractor.
Gone the old look that yoked him to the soil,
He's a new man now, part of the machine,
His nerves of metal and his blood oil.
The clutch curses, but the gears obey
His least bidding, and lo, he's away
Out of the farmyard, scattering hens.
Riding to work now as a great man should,
He is the knight at arms breaking the fields'
Mirror of silence, emptying the wood
Of foxes and squirrels and bright jays.
The sun comes over the tall trees
Kindling all the hedges, but not for him
Who runs his engine on a different fuel.
And all the birds are singing, bills wide in vain,
As Cynddylan passes proudly up the lane.

21 April • *from* The Old Vicarage, Grantchester • Rupert Brooke

Rupert Brooke wrote this sprightly poem while recuperating from a nervous breakdown in Berlin. It reflects upon his student days at the University of Cambridge, and the nearby village of Grantchester – a popular spot for students taking time out of their studies.

Ah God! to see the branches stir
Across the moon at Grantchester!
To smell the thrilling-sweet and rotten
Unforgettable, unforgotten
River-smell, and hear the breeze
Sobbing in the little trees.
Say, do the elm-clumps greatly stand
Still guardians of that holy land?
The chestnuts shade, in reverend dream,
The yet unacademic stream?
Is dawn a secret shy and cold
Anadyomene, silver-gold?
And sunset still a golden sea
From Haslingfield to Madingley?
And after, ere the night is born,
Do hares come out about the corn?
Oh, is the water sweet and cool,
Gentle and brown, above the pool?
And laughs the immortal river still
Under the mill, under the mill?
Say, is there Beauty yet to find?
And Certainty? and Quiet kind?

Deep meadows yet, for to forget
The lies, and truths, and pain? . . . oh! yet
Stands the Church clock at ten to three?
And is there honey still for tea?

21 April • In Memoriam (Easter 1915) • Edward Thomas

In these four lines, Edward Thomas reminds the reader of the waste of war. The poem was composed in April 1915, a few months before Thomas enlisted in the Artists Rifles.

The flowers left thick at nightfall in the wood
This Eastertide call into mind the men,
Now far from home, who, with their sweethearts, should
Have gathered them and will do never again.

22 April • The Woodspurge • Dante Gabriel Rossetti

The writer and artist Dante Gabriel Rossetti was the brother of the poet Christina Rossetti. This poem of his recounts a profound grief, where the speaker finds himself staring at a woodspurge, an evergreen that flowers from April to June.

The wind flapped loose, the wind was still,
Shaken out dead from tree and hill:
I had walked on at the wind's will, –
I sat now, for the wind was still.

Between my knees my forehead was, –
My lips, drawn in, said not Alas!
My hair was over in the grass,
My naked ears heard the day pass.

My eyes, wide open, had the run
Of some ten weeds to fix upon;
Among those few, out of the sun,
The woodspurge flowered, three cups in one.

From perfect grief there need not be
Wisdom or even memory:
One thing then learnt remains to me, –
The woodspurge has a cup of three.

22 April • A Dream within a Dream • Edgar Allan Poe

This work by the American poet Edgar Allan Poe takes as its subject the relationship between reality and fantasy.

Take this kiss upon the brow!
And, in parting from you now,
Thus much let me avow –
You are not wrong, who deem
That my days have been a dream;
Yet if hope has flown away
In a night, or in a day,
In a vision, or in none,
Is it therefore the less gone?
All that we see or seem
Is but a dream within a dream.

I stand amid the roar
Of a surf-tormented shore,
And I hold within my hand
Grains of the golden sand –
How few! yet how they creep
Through my fingers to the deep,
While I weep – while I weep!
O God! Can I not grasp
Them with a tighter clasp?
O God! can I not save
One from the pitiless wave?
Is all that we see or seem
But a dream within a dream?

23 April • *from* Richard II • William Shakespeare

Today is St George's Day, the feast day of the patron saint of England. It is also the traditional day of Shakespeare's birth in 1564 (and his death in 1616); records do not show when the Bard was born, but we know that he was baptized on 26 April 1564. These lines, from *Richard II*, bring together both days, in Shakespeare's tribute to the blessed plot of England.

This royal throne of kings, this sceptred isle,
This earth of majesty, this seat of Mars,
This other Eden, demi-paradise,
This fortress built by Nature for herself
Against infection and the hand of war;
This happy breed of men, this little world;
This precious stone set in the silver sea,
Which serves it in the office of a wall,
Or as a moat defensive to a house,
Against the envy of less happier lands;
This blessèd plot, this earth, this realm, this England.

23 April • Incident of the French Camp • Robert Browning

The Battle of Ratisbon took place on the 23 April 1809. It was fought as part of the Napoleonic Wars, between the French and Austrian empires. The poem focuses on an imagined exchange between a very young French soldier, fatally injured on his horse, and the Emperor Napoleon himself.

You know, we French storm'd Ratisbon:
 A mile or so away,
On a little mound, Napoleon
 Stood on our storming-day;
With neck out-thrust, you fancy how,
 Legs wide, arms lock'd behind,
As if to balance the prone brow
 Oppressive with its mind.

Just as perhaps he mused 'My plans
 That soar, to earth may fall,
Let once my army leader Lannes
 Waver at yonder wall,' –
Out 'twixt the battery-smokes there flew
 A rider, bound on bound
Full-galloping; nor bridle drew
 Until he reached the mound.

Then off there flung in smiling joy,
And held himself erect
By just his horse's mane, a boy:
You hardly could suspect –
(So tight he kept his lips compressed,
Scarce any blood came through)
You look'd twice ere you saw his breast
Was all but shot in two.

'Well,' cried he, 'Emperor, by God's grace
We've got you Ratisbon!
The Marshal's in the market-place,
And you'll be there anon
To see your flag-bird flap his vans
Where I, to heart's desire,
Perched him!' The chief's eye flash'd; his plans
Soared up again like fire.

The chief's eye flashed; but presently
Softened itself, as sheathes
A film the mother-eagle's eye
When her bruised eaglet breathes.
'You're wounded!' 'Nay,' the soldier's pride
Touch'd to the quick, he said:
'I'm kill'd, Sire!' And his chief beside
Smiling the boy fell dead.

24 April • Sonnet 18 • William Shakespeare

Shakespeare wrote 154 sonnets, but this one is perhaps his most well-known. Traditionally, sonnets have been associated with romantic love, often praising the virtues of the beloved.

Shall I compare thee to a summer's day?
Thou art more lovely and more temperate:
Rough winds do shake the darling buds of May,
And summer's lease hath all too short a date;
Sometime too hot the eye of heaven shines,
And often is his gold complexion dimm'd;
And every fair from fair sometime declines,
By chance, or nature's changing course, untrimm'd:
But thy eternal summer shall not fade,
Nor lose possession of that fair thou ow'st;
Nor shall death brag thou wander'st in his shade
When in eternal lines to time thou grow'st:
  So long as men can breathe or eyes can see,
  So long lives this, and this gives life to thee.

24 April • *from* The Tempest • William Shakespeare

The character of Caliban in Shakespeare's *The Tempest* is one of his most controversial and intriguing creations. While most of the characters deplore him as cruel and monstrous, Shakespeare, the master of antithesis, gives him these lines of a poet sensitive to the beauty of the island.

Be not afeard; the isle is full of noises,
Sounds and sweet airs, that give delight and hurt not.
Sometimes a thousand twangling instruments
Will hum about mine ears, and sometime voices
That, if I then had waked after long sleep,
Will make me sleep again: and then, in dreaming,
The clouds methought would open and show riches
Ready to drop upon me that, when I waked,
I cried to dream again.

25 April • Robinson Crusoe's Wise Sayings • Ian McMillan

Robinson Crusoe, popularly thought of as the very first English novel, was published this day in 1719. Written by Daniel Defoe, the book originally listed 'Robinson Crusoe' as its author, and, as the novel wasn't a familiar form of storytelling, it was read by many people as an authentic autobiography and travel journal. Ian McMillan's comic poem extracts wisdom from Robinson's hardships.

You can never have too many turtle eggs.
I'm the most interesting person in this room.
A beard is as long as I want it to be.

The swimmer on his own doesn't need trunks.
A tree is a good clock.
If you talk long enough to a rock you'll fall asleep.

I know it's Christmas because I cry.
Waving at ships is useless.
Footprints make me happy, unless they're my own.

25 April • *from* Henry VIII • William Shakespeare

This poem is taken from *Henry VIII*, a history play attributed to Shakespeare (as a collaboration, scholars now believe, with John Fletcher). The subject of the poem is the Greek mythical figure Orpheus and his divine power as a musician.

Orpheus with his lute made trees,
And the mountain tops that freeze,
Bow themselves when he did sing:
To his music plants and flowers
Ever sprung; as sun and showers
There had made a lasting spring.
Every thing that heard him play,
Even the billows of the sea,
Hung their heads, and then lay by.
In sweet music is such art,
Killing care and grief of heart
Fall asleep, or hearing, die.

26 April • Shakespeare • Matthew Arnold

Shakespeare is regarded by many as the most influential writer in the history of English literature. He even fundamentally altered the English language, inventing over 1,700 new words! Matthew Arnold, a highly regarded Victorian poet and critic, remembers Shakespeare in his own sonnet, published in 1849. Shakespeare's astonishing body of work has stood the test of time, and Matthew Arnold's sonnet is one of many love letters addressed to him, in the form made popular by the man himself.

Others abide our question. Thou art free.
We ask and ask – Thou smilest and art still,
Out-topping knowledge. For the loftiest hill,
Who to the stars uncrowns his majesty,

Planting his steadfast footsteps in the sea,
Making the heaven of heavens his dwelling-place,
Spares but the cloudy border of his base
To the foil'd searching of mortality;

And thou, who didst the stars and sunbeams know,
Self-school'd, self-scann'd, self-honour'd, self-secure,
Didst tread on earth unguess'd at. – Better so!

All pains the immortal spirit must endure,
All weakness which impairs, all griefs which bow,
Find their sole speech in that victorious brow.

26 April • Into my Heart an Air that Kills • A. E. Housman

This poem's rhetorical questions, about 'blue remembered hills', have become widely quoted. The poem is about the inaccessibility of memory and the past – we cannot get back to where we once were, but can only live our lives in the present.

Into my heart an air that kills
 From yon far country blows:
What are those blue remembered hills,
 What spires, what farms are those?

That is the land of lost content,
 I see it shining plain,
The happy highways where I went
 And cannot come again.

27 April • o by the by • E. E. Cummings

E. E. Cummings wrote around 2,900 poems, all unconventional, and all experimental. Many of his poems don't seem to make sense at all – but that's entirely intentional! Instead of trying to get everything to make sense, try just enjoying the flow of words and sounds. In this poem, being with someone is like flying your dreams as you would fly a kite.

o by the by
has anybody seen
little you-i
who stood on a green
hill and threw
his wish at blue

with a swoop and a dart
out flew his wish
(it dived like a fish
but it climbed like a dream)
throbbing like a heart
singing like a flame

blue took it my
far beyond far
and high beyond high
bluer took it your
but bluest took it our
away beyond where

what a wonderful thing
is the end of a string
(murmurs little you-i
as the hill becomes nil)
and will somebody tell
me why people let go

27 April • Child's Song in Spring • Edith Nesbit

Edith Nesbit was a poet and an author, and she wrote adventure stories such as *Five Children and It* and *The Railway Children*, but in this poem her inspiration comes from something more familiar – trees in spring.

The Silver Birch is a dainty lady,
She wears a satin gown;
The elm tree makes the old churchyard shady,
She will not live in town.

The English oak is a sturdy fellow,
He gets his green coat late;
The willow is smart in a suit of yellow
While brown the beech trees wait.

Such a gay green gown God gives the larches –
As green as he is good!
The hazels hold up their arms for arches,
When spring rides through the wood.

The chestnut's proud, and the lilac's pretty,
The poplar's gentle and tall,
But the plane tree's kind to the poor dull city –
I love him best of all!

28 April • Desiderata • Max Ehrmann

'Desiderata' is the most well-known work by the American poet Max Ehrmann. It is a prose poem – a type of writing, as you might expect, somewhere in between poetry and prose. So, while Ehrmann doesn't use rhyme or metre or regular stanza lengths, he does use the sort of language, imagery and metaphors we associate with poetry. Ehrmann's words offer advice and encouragement, both spiritual and practical, and at its centre are two words: 'Be yourself'.

Go placidly amid the noise and haste,
and remember what peace there may be in silence.
As far as possible without surrender
be on good terms with all persons.
Speak your truth quietly and clearly;
and listen to others,
even the dull and the ignorant;
they too have their story.

Avoid loud and aggressive persons,
they are vexations to the spirit.
If you compare yourself with others,
you may become vain and bitter;
for always there will be greater and lesser persons than
    yourself.
Enjoy your achievements as well as your plans.

Keep interested in your own career, however humble;
it is a real possession in the changing fortunes of time.
Exercise caution in your business affairs;

for the world is full of trickery.
But let this not blind you to what virtue there is;
many persons strive for high ideals;
and everywhere life is full of heroism.

Be yourself.
Especially, do not feign affection.
Neither be cynical about love;
for in the face of all aridity and disenchantment
it is as perennial as the grass.

Take kindly the counsel of the years,
gracefully surrendering the things of youth.
Nurture strength of spirit to shield you in sudden
misfortune.
But do not distress yourself with dark imaginings.
Many fears are born of fatigue and loneliness.
Beyond a wholesome discipline,
be gentle with yourself.

You are a child of the universe,
no less than the trees and the stars;
you have a right to be here.
And whether or not it is clear to you,
no doubt the universe is unfolding as it should.

Therefore be at peace with God,
whatever you conceive Him to be,
and whatever your labors and aspirations,
in the noisy confusion of life keep peace with your soul.

With all its sham, drudgery, and broken dreams,
it is still a beautiful world.
Be cheerful.
Strive to be happy.

28 April • Nostos • Louise Glück

The great American poet Louise Glück received the 2020 Nobel Prize in Literature 'for her unmistakable poetic voice that, with austere beauty, makes individual existence universal'. That is certainly the case for this wonderfully poignant poem which follows her personal reflections on the natural surroundings that defined her childhood, before inviting us, with a unifying 'we', to share in an observation about our collective perceptions and memories.

There was an apple tree in the yard —
this would have been
forty years ago – behind,
only meadows. Drifts
of crocus in the damp grass.
I stood at that window:
late April. Spring
flowers in the neighbor's yard.
How many times, really, did the tree
flower on my birthday,
the exact day, not
before, not after? Substitution
of the immutable
for the shifting, the evolving.
Substitution of the image
for relentless earth. What
do I know of this place,
the role of the tree for decades
taken by a bonsai, voices
rising from the tennis courts —
Fields. Smell of the tall grass, new cut.

As one expects of a lyric poet.
We look at the world once, in childhood.
The rest is memory.

29 April • Dancing with Life • Shauna Darling Robertson

29 April is International Dance Day, in global celebration of the art of dance – from tap-dance to tango, and ballet to breakdance.

I beckoned to the floor
missed buses and lost races.
We body-popped till sore.

I held out my hand
to every failed exam.
We lindy-hopped. We can-canned.

I slipped my arm around the waist
of *chicken, loser, nerd.*
We skip-jived at a pace.

I chose the longest, dullest week
and pressed it to my chest
as we cha-cha'd cheek to cheek.

I tipped and doffed my hat
to a hundred horrid haircuts.
We mambo'd, tango'd, tapped.

Feeling bold, I turned to face
my darkest, rawest faults.
I took them in my arms, we bowed
and broke into a waltz.

29 April • The Emperor's Rhyme • A. A. Milne

This jaunty poem features a fair amount of rhyming, which makes it easy to learn off by heart. Just don't try to do the sums in your head!

The King of Peru
(Who was Emperor too)
  Had a sort of a rhyme
    Which was useful to know,
If he felt very shy
When a stranger came by,
  Or they asked him the time
    When his watch didn't go;
or supposing he fell
(By mistake) down the well,
  Or he tumbled when skating
    And sat on his hat,
Or perhaps wasn't told,
  Till his porridge was cold,
    That his breakfast was waiting –
Or something like that;

Oh, whenever the Emperor
got into a temper, or
  Felt himself sulky or sad,
He would murmur and murmur,
Until he felt firmer,
  This curious rhyme which he had:

'Eight eights are sixty-four;
Multiply by seven.
When it's done,
Carry one,
And take away eleven.
Nine nines are eighty-one;
Multiply by three.
If it's more,
Carry four,
And then it's time for tea.'

So whenever the Queen
Took his armour to clean,
And didn't remember
To use any starch;
Or his birthday (in May)
Was a horrible day,
Being wet as November
And windy as March;
Or, if sitting in state
With the Wise and the Great
He happened to hiccup
While signing his name,
Or The Queen gave a cough,
When his crown tumbled off
As he bent down to pick up
A pen for the same;

Oh, whenever the Emperor
Got into a temper, or
Felt himself awkward or shy,
He would whisper and whisper,
Until he felt crisper,
This odd little rhyme to the sky.

'Eight eights are eighty-one;
Multiply by seven.
When it's done,
Carry one,
And take away eleven.
Nine nines are sixty-four;
Multiply by three.
When it's done,
Carry one,
And then it's time for tea.'

30 April • The Hippopotamus's Birthday • E. V. Rieu

Although E. V. Rieu was best known for his hugely successful translation of *The Odyssey*, his humorous poetry for children suggests that he didn't spend all of his time on the classics.

He has opened all his parcels
  but the largest and the last;
His hopes are at their highest
  and his heart is beating fast.
O happy Hippopotamus,
  what lovely gift is here?
He cuts the string. The world stands still.
  A pair of boots appear!

O little Hippopotamus,
  the sorrows of the small!
He dropped two tears to mingle
  with the flowing Senegal;
And the 'Thank you' that he uttered
  was the saddest ever heard
In the Senegambian jungle
  from the mouth of beast or bird.

30 April • Facing It • Yusef Komunyakaa

On 30 April 1975, Saigon, the capital of South Vietnam, was captured by Northern Vietnamese forces. This event, known as the Fall of Saigon, marked the defeat of South Vietnam and the US forces which supported them, and ended the Vietnam War – a conflict which had raged for nearly twenty years and resulted in the deaths of approximately four million people. This poem is set inside the Vietnam Veterans Memorial, which honours the American soldiers who lost their lives in the war.

My black face fades,
hiding inside the black granite.
I said I wouldn't,
dammit: No tears.
I'm stone. I'm flesh.
My clouded reflection eyes me
like a bird of prey, the profile of night
slanted against morning. I turn
this way – the stone lets me go.
I turn that way – I'm inside
the Vietnam Veterans Memorial
again, depending on the light
to make a difference.
I go down the 58,022 names,
half-expecting to find
my own in letters like smoke.
I touch the name Andrew Johnson;
I see the booby trap's white flash.
Names shimmer on a woman's blouse
but when she walks away

the names stay on the wall.
Brushstrokes flash, a red bird's
wings cutting across my stare.
The sky. A plane in the sky.
A white vet's image floats
closer to me, then his pale eyes
look through mine. I'm a window.
He's lost his right arm
inside the stone. In the black mirror
a woman's trying to erase names:
No, she's brushing a boy's hair.

May

1 May • Verses said to be written on the Union • Jonathan Swift

On 1 May 1707, the Acts of Union between England and Scotland were passed, forming modern Great Britain. Queen Anne was on the throne at the time, and Jonathan Swift, a satirist, produced the following lines.

The Queen has lately lost a Part
Of her entirely-*English* Heart,
For want of which, by way of Botch,
She piec'd it up again with *Scotch*.
Blest Revolution, which creates
Divided Hearts, united States.
See how the double Nation lies;
Like a rich Coat with Skirts of Frize:
As if a Man in making Posies
Should bundle Thistles up with Roses.
Who ever yet a Union saw
Of Kingdoms, without Faith or Law.
Henceforward let no Statesman dare,
A Kingdom, to a Ship compare;
Lest he should call our Commonweal
A Vessel with a double Keel:
Which just like ours, new rigg'd and mann'd,
And got about a League from Land,
By Change of Wind to Leeward Side
The Pilot knew not how to guide.
So tossing Faction will o'erwhelm
Our crazy double-bottom'd Realm.

1 May • May Day • Sara Teasdale

1 May, known as May Day, marks an ancient festival dating back to the pre-Christian era. Traditional English activities associated with the day include morris dancing, the crowning of a May Queen to lead the festival celebrations, and dancing around a maypole. This poem by the American poet Sara Teasdale celebrates the beauty of nature on May Day – even in a city.

The shining line of motors,
The swaying motor-bus,
The prancing dancing horses
Are passing by for us.

The sunlight on the steeple,
The toys we stop to see,
The smiling passing people
Are all for you and me.

'I love you and I love you!'—
'And oh, I love you, too!'
'All of the flower girl's lilies
Were only grown for you!'

Fifth Avenue and April
And love and lack of care—
The world is mad with music
Too beautiful to bear.

2 May • The Merry Month of May • Thomas Dekker

Thomas Dekker was a poet and playwright during the Elizabethan and Jacobean era. This poem overflows with praise for bright May days.

O! the month of May, the merry month of May,
  So frolic, so gay, and so green, so green, so green!
O! and then did I unto my true Love say,
  Sweet Peg, thou shalt be my Summer's Queen.

Now the nightingale, the pretty nightingale,
  The sweetest singer in all the forest choir,
Entreats thee, sweet Peggy, to hear thy true love's tale:
  Lo! yonder she sitteth, her breast against a briar.

But O! I spy the cuckoo, the cuckoo, the cuckoo;
  See where she sitteth; come away, my joy:
Come away, I prithee, I do not like the cuckoo
  Should sing where my Peggy and I kiss and toy.

O! the month of May, the merry month of May,
  So frolic, so gay, and so green, so green, so green!
And then did I unto my true Love say,
  Sweet Peg, thou shalt be my Summer's Queen.

2 May • Leisure • W. H. Davies

Sometimes we are so busy that we forget to look up and notice the glories of nature.

What is this life if, full of care,
We have no time to stand and stare?

No time to stand beneath the boughs
And stare as long as sheep or cows.

No time to see, when woods we pass,
Where squirrels hide their nuts in grass.

No time to see, in broad daylight,
Streams full of stars, like skies at night.

No time to turn at Beauty's glance,
And watch her feet, how they can dance.

No time to wait till her mouth can
Enrich that smile her eyes began.

A poor life this is if, full of care,
We have no time to stand and stare.

3 May • Tartary • Walter de la Mare

'Tartary' is a historical region that covers most of Russia, northern China and stretches down to India – but it's a word that hasn't been commonly used in centuries. In this poem, de la Mare imagines Tartary as a beautiful and fantastical land, and even goes as far as to imagine himself as its ruler!

If I were Lord of Tartary,
  Myself, and me alone,
My bed should be of ivory,
  Of beaten gold my throne;
And in my court should peacocks flaunt,
And in my forests tigers haunt,
And in my pools great fishes slant
  Their fins athwart the sun.

If I were Lord of Tartary,
  Trumpeters every day
To all my meals should summon me,
  And in my courtyards bray;
And in the evening lamps should shine,
Yellow as honey, red as wine,
While harp, and flute, and mandoline
  Made music sweet and gay.

If I were Lord of Tartary,
  I'd wear a robe of beads,
White, and gold, and green they'd be –
  And small and thick as seeds;
And ere should wane the morning star,
I'd don my robe and scimitar.
And zebras seven should draw my car
  Through Tartary's dark glades.

Lord of the fruits of Tartary,
  Her rivers silver-pale!
Lord of the hills of Tartary,
  Glen, thicket, wood, and dale!
Her flashing stars, her scented breeze,
Her trembling lakes, like foamless seas,
Her bird-delighting citron-trees,
  In every purple vale!

3 May • The Fawn • Edna St Vincent Millay

Edna St Vincent Millay is considered a great nature poet, and in this poem she describes a moment in which she comes upon a fawn on a 'forest day'.

There it was I saw what I shall never forget
And never retrieve.
Monstrous and beautiful to human eyes, hard to believe,
He lay, yet there he lay,
Asleep on the moss, his head on his polished cleft small
   ebony hooves,
The child of the doe, the dappled child of the deer.

Surely his mother had never said, 'Lie here
Till I return,' so spotty and plain to see
On the green moss lay he.
His eyes had opened; he considered me.
I would have given more than I care to say
To thrifty ears, might I have had him for my friend
One moment only of that forest day:

Might I have had the acceptance, not the love
Of those clear eyes;
Might I have been for him in the bough above
Or the root beneath his forest bed,
A part of the forest, seen without surprise.

Was it alarm, or was it the wind of my fear lest he depart
That jerked him to his jointy knees,
And sent him crashing off, leaping and stumbling
On his new legs, between the stems of the white trees?

4 May • Back in the Playground Blues • Adrian Mitchell

Today is the United Nations' Anti-Bullying Day – a day which raises awareness of the damaging effects of this behaviour. The pain of being bullied is powerfully evoked in Adrian Mitchell's poem.

I dreamed I was back in the playground, I was about four feet high
Yes I dreamed I was back in the playground, standing about four feet high
Well the playground was three miles long and the playground was five miles wide
It was broken black tarmac with a high wire fence all around
Broken black dusty tarmac with a high fence running all around
And it had a special name to it, they called it The Killing Ground

Got a mother and a father they're one thousand years away
The rulers of The Killing Ground are coming out to play
Everybody thinking: 'Who they going to play with today?'

Well you get it for being Jewish
And you get it for being black
Get it for being chicken
Get it for fighting back
You get it for being big and fat
Get it for being small
O those who get it get it and get it
For any damn thing at all

Sometimes they take a beetle, tear off its six legs one by one
Beetle on its black back, rocking in the lunchtime sun
But a beetle can't beg for mercy, a beetle's not half the fun

Heard a deep voice talking, it had that iceberg sound,
'It prepares them for Life' – but I have never found
Any place in my life that's worse than The Killing Ground.

4 May • Old Pond • Matsuo Bashō, translated by Robert Hass

In Japan, 4 May is known as *Midori no hi* – a day for the celebration of nature. Japanese haikus, such as this one by the revered poet Matsuo Bashō, traditionally focus on an element of the natural world.

The old pond –
a frog jumps in,
sound of water.

5 May • Clouds • Matsuo Bashō, translated by Robert Hass

This is another haiku by Bashō, and like 'Old Pond' it uses very simple imagery to great effect.

From time to time
The clouds give rest
To the moon-beholders.

5 May • The Song of the Banana Man • Evan Jones

'The Song of the Banana Man' was published as part of the celebrations of Jamaica's independence in 1962, although Jones wrote it in the fifties after some fellow students at Oxford asserted that no poem of quality could ever be written in anything other than 'proper' English. It has since become one of the most loved poems across the whole of the Caribbean, and is considered a modern song of Jamaican identity.

Touris', white man, wipin' his face,
Met me in Golden Grove market place.
He looked at m' ol' clothes brown wid stain,
An' soaked right through wid de Portlan' rain,
He cas' his eye, turn' up his nose,
He says, 'You're a beggar man, I suppose?'
He says, 'Boy, get some occupation,
Be of some value to your nation.'

I said, 'By God and dis big right han'
You mus' recognize a banana man.

'Up in de hills, where de streams are cool,
An' mullet an' janga swim in de pool,
I have ten acres of mountain side,
An' a dainty-foot donkey dat I ride,
Four Gros Michel, an' four Lacatan,
Some coconut trees, and some hills of yam,
An' I pasture on dat very same lan'
Five she-goats an' a big black ram,

'Dat, by God an' dis big right han'
Is de property of a banana man.

'I leave m' yard early-mornin' time
An' set m' foot to de mountain climb,
I ben m' back to de hot-sun toil,
An' m' cutlass rings on de stony soil,
Ploughin' an' weedin', diggin' an' plantin',
Till Massa Sun drop back o' John Crow mountain,
Den home again in cool evenin' time,
Perhaps whistling dis likkle rhyme,

'Praise God an' m' big right han'
I will live an' die a banana man.

'Banana day is my special day,
I cut my stems an' I'm on m' way,
Load up de donkey, leave de lan'
Head down de hill to banana stan',
When de truck comes roun' I take a ride
All de way down to de harbour side –
Dat is de night, when you, touris' man,
Would change your place wid a banana man.

'Yes, by God, an' m' big right han'
I will live an' die a banana man.

'De bay is calm, an' de moon is bright
De hills look black for de sky is light,
Down at de dock is an English ship,
Restin' after her ocean trip,
While on de pier is a monstrous hustle,
Tallymen, carriers, all in a bustle,

Wid stems on deir heads in a long black snake
Some singin' de sons dat banana men make,

'Like, Praise God an' m' big right han'
I will live an' die a banana man.

'Den de payment comes, an' we have some fun,
Me, Zekiel, Bredda and Duppy Son.
Down at de bar near United Wharf
We knock back a white rum, bus' a laugh,
Fill de empty bag for further toil
Wid saltfish, breadfruit, coconut oil.
Den head back home to m' yard to sleep,
A proper sleep dat is long an' deep.

'Yes, by God, an' m' big right han'
I will live an' die a banana man.

'So when you see dese ol' clothes brown wid stain,
An' soaked right through wid de Portlan' rain,
Don't cas' your eye nor turn your nose,
Don't judge a man by his patchy clothes,
I'm a strong man, a proud man, an' I'm free,
Free as dese mountains, free as dis sea,
I know myself, an' I know my ways,
An' will sing wid pride to de end o' my days

'Praise God an' m' big right han'
I will live an' die a banana man.'

6 May • Buckingham Palace • A. A. Milne

George V was proclaimed king on this day in 1910 and reigned over Britain until his death in 1936. This poem by A. A. Milne was written in 1924; George V was only the second monarch after his grandmother Queen Victoria to reside in Buckingham Palace. A. A. Milne is better known as the author of *Winnie-the-Pooh*, but Pooh's fictional friend Christopher Robin – also the name of Milne's son – features here as well.

They're changing guard at Buckingham Palace –
Christopher Robin went down with Alice.
Alice is marrying one of the guard.
'A soldier's life is terrible hard,'
Says Alice.

They're changing guard at Buckingham Palace –
Christopher Robin went down with Alice.
We saw a guard in a sentry-box.
'One of the sergeants looks after their socks,'
Says Alice.

They're changing guard at Buckingham Palace –
Christopher Robin went down with Alice.
We looked for the King, but he never came.
'Well, God take care of him, all the same,'
Says Alice.

They're changing guard at Buckingham Palace –
Christopher Robin went down with Alice.
They've great big parties inside the grounds.
'I wouldn't be King for a hundred pounds,'
Says Alice.

They're changing guard at Buckingham Palace –
Christopher Robin went down with Alice.
A face looked out, but it wasn't the King's.
'He's much too busy a-signing things,'
Says Alice.

They're changing guard at Buckingham Palace –
Christopher Robin went down with Alice.
'Do you think the King knows all about me?'
'Sure to, dear, but it's time for tea,'
Says Alice.

6 May • To a Squirrel at Kyle-Na-No • W. B. Yeats

'To a Squirrel' was inspired by a visit to the wood of Kyle-na-no in Coole Park, County Galway. W. B. Yeats lived just three miles from the park, and several of his poems were inspired by experiences in the nature reserve.

Come play with me;
Why should you run
Through the shaking tree
As though I'd a gun
To strike you dead?
When all I would do
Is to scratch your head
And let you go.

7 May • The Pobble Who Has No Toes • Edward Lear

Another slice of nonsense verse from Edward Lear. This poem features a 'Runcible Cat'; Lear actually made up the word 'runcible', and seemed to like it a lot, as he used it frequently (there is a 'runcible spoon' in 'The Owl and the Pussycat'). It even appears in the *Oxford English Dictionary*, defined as simply 'a nonsense word'.

I

The Pobble who has no toes
    Had once as many as we;
When they said, 'Some day you may lose them all;' –
    He replied, – 'Fish fiddle de-dee!'
And his Aunt Jobiska made him drink,
Lavender water tinged with pink,
For she said, 'The World in general knows
There's nothing so good for a Pobble's toes!'

II

The Pobble who has no toes,
    Swam across the Bristol Channel;
But before he set out he wrapped his nose,
    In a piece of scarlet flannel.
For his Aunt Jobiska said, 'No harm
Can come to his toes if his nose is warm;
And it's perfectly known that a Pobble's toes
Are safe, – provided he minds his nose.'

III

The Pobble swam fast and well
    And when boats or ships came near him
He tinkedly-binkledy-winkled a bell
    So that all the world could hear him.
And all the Sailors and Admirals cried,
When they saw him nearing the further side, –
'He has gone to fish, for his Aunt Jobiska's
Runcible Cat with crimson whiskers!'

IV

But before he touched the shore,
    The shore of the Bristol Channel,
A sea-green Porpoise carried away
    His wrapper of scarlet flannel.
And when he came to observe his feet
Formerly garnished with toes so neat
His face at once became forlorn
On perceiving that all his toes were gone!

V

And nobody ever knew
    From that dark day to the present,
Whoso had taken the Pobble's toes,
    In a manner so far from pleasant.
Whether the shrimps or crawfish gray,
Or crafty Mermaids stole them away –
Nobody knew; and nobody knows
How the Pobble was robbed of his twice five toes!

VI

The Pobble who has no toes
    Was placed in a friendly Bark,
And they rowed him back, and carried him up,
    To his Aunt Jobiska's Park.
And she made him a feast at his earnest wish
Of eggs and buttercups fried with fish; –
And she said, – 'It's a fact the whole world knows,
That Pobbles are happier without their toes.'

7 May • You Ain't Nothing but a Hedgehog • John Cooper Clarke

The performance poet John Cooper Clarke's witty poem is a rewriting of a blues song, 'Hound Dog', famously recorded in 1956 by the King of Rock and Roll, Elvis Presley.

You ain't nothing but a hedgehog
Foragin' all the time
You ain't nothing but a hedgehog
Foragin' all the time
You ain't never pricked a predator
You ain't no porcupine.

8 May • Why the Bat Flies at Night • Roger Stevens

Like John Cooper Clarke's reimagining of a hedgehog as a rock 'n' roll figure, this work by the contemporary poet Roger Stevens gives us a completely new perspective on a familiar animal.

Once, when the moon was as bright as the sun
And the stars lit up the sky
And the day and the night were both as one,
The bat came flying by

The bat flew by fast and furious
And attached to his back with string
Was a basket. The animals were curious
They said, Bat, what is in that thing?

Ah, said the bat, well, this afternoon
I was given a task to do
To take this basket up to the moon
But what's in it? I haven't a clue.

But the bat was no long-distance flyer
And he had to lie down for a sleep
So, due to the others' insistence,
The lion opened the basket to peep

Then all at once from the basket
There came a most terrible sight
A shadow that fell like a dark net
Bringing the blackness of night

And that is why bats rise at twilight
And they sleep through the bright hours of day
Why they chivvy and chase the dark slivers of night
The darkness they let get away

8 May • Impromptu on Charles II • John Wilmot, Earl of Rochester

On this day in 1660, Parliament met to restore Charles II to the throne of England, Scotland and Ireland. A lover of wine, women and the arts, became known as 'the Merry Monarch'. One court favourite was John Wilmot, Earl of Rochester, an entertaining writer of bawdy poems. However, he pushed his luck too far with this poem, which he is said to have handed to the king himself. Charles was insensed and Rochester was henceforth banned from his court.

God bless our good and gracious King
Whose promise none relyes on
Who never said A foolish thing
Nor ever did A wise one.

9 May • What the teacher said when asked: What er we avin for geography, Miss? • John Agard

The Greek astronomer Hipparchus, in the second century BC, was the first person to understand location in terms of longitude and latitude – necessary coordinates for all sea travel and exploration. The student in Agard's poem, though, journeys by another means, by dreaming his class away.

This morning I've got too much energy
much too much for geography

I'm in a high mood
so class don't think me crude
but you can stuff latitude and longitude

I've had enough of the earth's crust
today I want to touch the clouds

Today I want to sing out loud
and tear all maps to shreds

I'm not settling for river beds
I want the sky and nothing less

Today I couldn't care if east turns west
Today I've got so much energy
I could do press-ups on the desk
but that won't take much out of me

Today I'll dance on the globe
In a rainbow robe

while you class remain seated

on your natural zone
with your pens and things
watching my contours grow wings

All right, class, see you later.
If the headmaster asks for me
say I'm a million dreaming degrees
beyond the equator

a million dreaming degrees
beyond the equator

9 May • Mayfly • Mary Ann Hoberman

People have always been fascinated by the brief lives of mayflies. Hatching in vast numbers on warm spring days, these insects often live only for a single day! We might find in the poem a message about the fragility and preciousness of all life.

Think how fast a year flies by
A month flies by
A week flies by
Think how fast a day flies by
A Mayfly's life lasts but a day
A single day
To live and die
A single day
How fast it goes
The day
The Mayfly
Both of those.
A Mayfly flies a single day
The daylight dies and darkness grows
A single day
How fast it flies
A Mayfly's life
How fast it goes.

10 May • For my Niece • Kae Tempest

Kae Tempest is a performance poet and rapper, living and working in London. His poetry, which is direct and modern in style, is nevertheless inspired by poets across the history of English literature.

I hold you in my arms,
your age is told in months.

There's things I hope you'll learn.
Things I'm sure that I learned once.

But there's nothing I can teach you.
You'll find all that you need.

No flower bends its head to offer
teaching to a seed.

The seed will grow and blossom
once the flower's ground to dust.

But even so, if nothing else,
one thing I'll entrust:

Doing what you please
is not the same

as doing what you must.

10 May • Brother • Mary Ann Hoberman

This poem by Mary Ann Hoberman feels almost like a tongue-twister in its repetitions of 'bother' and 'brother' so close together.

I had a little brother
And I brought him to my mother
And I said I want another
Little brother for a change.
But she said don't be a bother
So I took him to my father
And I said this little bother
Of a brother's very strange.
But he said one little brother
Is exactly like another
And every little brother
Misbehaves a bit he said.
So I took the little bother
From my mother and my father
And I put the little bother
Of a brother back to bed.

11 May • *from* Doctor Faustus • Christopher Marlowe

Christopher Marlowe was one of the greatest writers in history, though, thanks to Shakespeare, he is remembered as only the second greatest playwright of the Elizabethan age. Marlowe's *Doctor Faustus* is based on a German folk tale about a brilliant young man who sells his soul to the devil in exchange for knowledge and pleasure. In this scene, Faustus is presented by the devil with the mythical Helen of Troy, who was said to be the most beautiful woman ever to have lived. Her abduction led to the Trojan War.

Was this the face that launch'd a thousand ships,
And burnt the topless towers of Ilium?
Sweet Helen, make me immortal with a kiss.
Her lips suck forth my soul; see, where it flies! –
Come, Helen, come, give me my soul again.
Here will I dwell, for Heaven be in these lips,
And all is dross that is not Helena.
I will be Paris, and for love of thee,
Instead of Troy, shall Wittenberg be sack'd;
And I will combat with weak Menelaus,
And wear thy colours on my plumèd crest;
Yea, I will wound Achilles in the heel,
And then return to Helen for a kiss.
O, thou art fairer than the evening air
Clad in the beauty of a thousand stars;
Brighter art thou than flaming Jupiter
When he appear'd to hapless Semele;
More lovely than the monarch of the sky
In wanton Arethusa's azur'd arms;
And none but thou shalt be my paramour.

11 May • The Selkie Bride • Tony Mitton

The subject of this poem is the mythological selkie – a creature that resembles a seal in the water but a human on land. Legends involving the selkie can be found in Scottish, Irish and Icelandic folklore. Tony Mitton's poem tells the story of young Donallan, who falls in love with a selkie.

Young Donallan lived alone
with the sound of the sea and the wind's wild moan,
and the hiss of the kettle, the sigh of the peat,
with a cat in his lap and a dog at his feet.

Young Donallan spread his net.
He landed the fish that he could get.
He grew his cabbage in a scant croft patch,
and he caulked his boat and he roped his thatch.

On the seventh day of the high Spring tide
His heart grew full and he stretched and sighed.
So he walked the length of the lonely strand
To the chafe of the surf on the soft sea sand.

Young Donallan tuned his ear
to the cry of the gulls on the salt sea air.
But above the birds and the fall of the flood
there rose a sound that swelled his blood.

Down on the rocks a selkie sang,
And he drank the song till his senses rang.
He gazed at the sight of her glimmering there
With her graceful form and her winnowing hair.

He knew the lore and the ways of old
From the talk, and the tales his father told.
So he seized the skin that lay by her side,
Crying, 'Selkie, I take you to be my bride.'

She begged for the skin, on her bended knee,
for without it she could not return to the sea.
But her eyes were dark and her skin was soft,
and Donallan led her back to his croft.

Young Donallan and his selkie bride
lived in the croft to the tune of the tide,
She stitched his shirt and she baked his bread
And she lay by his side in the old box bed.

She bore him children, one, two, three.
Their eyes were as soft as the seals' of the sea.
They loved their mother with her gentle ways
But they knew her sigh and her sad sea gaze.

And they felt in their hearts there was something wrong
for her voice was sweet but she sang no song.
Whenever she soothed them to sleep at night
Her eyes were kind but her lips pressed tight.

It was on a day when the wind was wild
and Donallan was out with the eldest child,
that the Selkie Bride was baking bread
when all of a sudden the youngest said,

'Early this morning while the family slept
I followed our father out where he crept.
He loosened a stone in the old croft wall
And he took from the hollow a sleek grey caul.

'He oiled and smoothed that supple skin,
Then he folded it tight and put it back in.
Now tell me, Mother, oh spell to me
the meaning of this mystery.'

But his mother, never a word she said.
She found the skin and she left her bread.
Then she led the children to the edge of the land
where the waters lap at the silver sand.

'Now, listen, my dears, oh listen to me.
Your mother's home is here in the sea.
It was here in Spring, at the height of the tide,
Your father took me to be his bride.

'And though it tear at your mother's heart,
it's here on the shore that we must part.'
She shook her skin and she put it on.
Then she fell to the waves and she was gone.

When they told their father, he scarcely stirred.
He gave a sigh, but he spoke no word.
For he knew that a selkie, such as she,
must come at last to her home in the sea.

So Donallan lived in the small thatched croft,
with his children three and their eyes so soft.
But whenever in Spring the tides rose high
And a round moon rode in the cool night sky,

they would hear the music, clear and strong,
the sound of their mother's selkie song,
and they knew she was near, in the swing of the sea,
where the waters roll and the seal swim free.

And from that time, in the midst of the storm,
they were safe from the waves that spoil and harm.
And whoever was of their selkie brood,
their boats stayed sound and their catch was good.

12 May • Silkie • Dave Calder

This poem by Dave Calder also takes the mythological selkie, spelt here as 'silkie', as its subject. The poet here pairs the transformation between human and selkie form with the transition between being awake and falling asleep.

The gulls had quietened on the chimneypots
and in the unending dusk of the summer night
he could hear the sea pushing and pulling at pebbles, in and
    out, rise and fall,
and when he slid into the sheets they felt
as smooth and cool as slipping into water
down down
until only his head only his nose and eyes
bobbed above water and then
his body losing all sense of weight so
sleek skinned sinking deeper
into the pulse of the sea breathing
rise and fall, in and out, down down
deep and far the song of whales sounding

When he woke, the sheets were a tangle
of breakers, he lay beached on the bed, his head resting on
    the small white sandbank, the gulls wheeling against the
    sunlight

12 May • On a Lane in Spring • John Clare

Sonnets usually involve some sort of tension or change of directions, especially in the final couplet. But in Clare's sonnet on spring there is no such tension. The poem moves harmoniously from natural form to natural form, and ends with a complete image of springtime in a country lane. In this way, Clare uses the form of the sonnet to create an unexpectedly tranquil picture.

A little lane – the brook runs close beside,
    And spangles in the sunshine, while the fish glide
        swiftly by;
And hedges leafing with the green springtide;
    From out their greenery the old birds fly,
And chirp and whistle in the morning sun;
    The pilewort glitters 'neath the pale blue sky,
The little robin has its nest begun
    The grass-green linnets round the bushes fly.
How mild the spring comes in! the daisy buds
    Lift up their golden blossoms to the sky.
    How lovely are the pingles and the woods!
    Here a beetle runs – and there a fly
Rests on the arum leaf in bottle-green,
And all the spring in this sweet lane is seen.

13 May • The Lanyard • Billy Collins

Though Mothering Sunday has been and gone in the UK, Mother's Day in the USA takes place on the second Sunday in May. The American poet Billy Collins thinks about the impossible debt we owe to our mothers, through a gift he gave his mother: a home-made lanyard. The reference to a 'French novelist' and memory is to Marcel Proust's *In Search of Lost Time* – a novel in which a bite of a madeleine, a little French cake, brings back a torrent of memories.

The other day as I was ricocheting slowly
off the blue walls of this room,
bouncing from typewriter to piano,
from bookshelf to an envelope lying on the floor,
I found myself in the L section of the dictionary
where my eyes fell upon the word *lanyard*.

No cookie nibbled by a French novelist
could send one more suddenly into the past –
a past where I sat at a workbench at a camp
by a deep Adirondack lake
learning how to braid long thin plastic strips
into a lanyard, a gift for my mother.

I had never seen anyone use a lanyard
or wear one, if that's what you did with them,
but that did not keep me from crossing
strand over strand again and again
until I had made a boxy
red and white lanyard for my mother.

She gave me life and milk from her breasts,
and I gave her a lanyard.
She nursed me in many a sick room,
lifted spoons of medicine to my lips,
laid cold face-cloths on my forehead,
and then led me out into the airy light

and taught me to walk and swim,
and I, in turn, presented her with a lanyard.
Here are thousands of meals, she said,
and here is clothing and a good education.
And here is your lanyard, I replied,
which I made with a little help from a counselor.

Here is a breathing body and a beating heart,
strong legs, bones and teeth,
and two clear eyes to read the world, she whispered,
and here, I said, is the lanyard I made at camp.
And here, I wish to say to her now,
is a smaller gift – not the archaic truth

that you can never repay your mother,
but the rueful admission that when she took
the two-tone lanyard from my hands,
I was as sure as a boy could be
that this useless, worthless thing I wove
out of boredom would be enough to make us even.

13 May • Swan and Shadow • John Hollander

With its beautiful and startlingly symmetrical appearance, this poem is one of the most celebrated examples of a picture poem.

Dusk
Above the
water hang the
loud
flies
Here
O so
gray
then
What   A pale signal will appear
When   Soon before its shadow fades
Where   Here in this pool of opened eye
In us   No Upon us As at the very edges
of where we take shape in the dark air
this object bares its image awakening
ripples of recognition that will
brush darkness up into light
even after this bird this hour both drift by atop the perfect sad instant now
already passing out of sight
toward yet-untroubled reflection
this image bears its object darkening
into memorial shades Scattered bits of
Light   No of water Or something across
water   Breaking up No Being regathered
Soon   Yet by then a swan will have
gone   Yes Out of mind into what
vast
pale
hush
of a
place
past
sudden dark as
if a swan
sang

14 May • Rondeau • Leigh Hunt

The 'rondeau' is a poetic form originating in medieval France. It is a lyrical form, designed to be set to music and sung, and its name signifies that it goes 'around' – it returns to where it began.

Jenny kissed me when we met,
  Jumping from the chair she sat in;
Time, you thief, who love to get
  Sweets into your list, put that in:
Say I'm weary, say I'm sad,
  Say that health and wealth have missed me,
Say I'm growing old, but add
  Jenny kissed me.

14 May • Love You More • James Carter

It is difficult to tell somebody how much you love them, and in this poem James Carter uses increasingly enormous metaphors to try to measure his emotions.

Do I love you
to the moon and back?
No I love you
more than that
I love you to the desert sands
the mountains, stars
the planets and
I love you to the deepest sea
and deeper still
through history
Before beyond I love you then
I love you now
I'll love you when
The sun's gone out
the moon's gone home
and all the stars are fully grown
When I no longer say these words
I'll give them to the wind, the birds
so that they will still be heard
I love you

15 May • I Found a Ball of Grass among the Hay • John Clare

John Clare was the son of a farm labourer, and he is noted for his poems that celebrate the English countryside.

I found a ball of grass among the hay
And progged it as I passed and went away;
And when I looked I fancied something stirred,
And turned again and hoped to catch the bird—
When out an old mouse bolted in the wheats
With all her young ones hanging at her teats;
She looked so odd and so grotesque to me,
I ran and wondered what the thing could be,
And pushed the knapweed bunches where I stood;
Then the mouse hurried from the craking brood.
The young ones squeaked, and as I went away
She found her nest again among the hay.
The water o'er the pebbles scarce could run
And broad old cesspools glittered in the sun.

15 May • *from* The Love Song of J. Alfred Prufrock • T. S. Eliot

These lines are from the beginning of one of Eliot's greatest poems. Many beautiful lines from 'The Love Song of J. Alfred Prufrock' have become famous – and you only have to read it aloud to hear why! It is the story, sometimes sad, sometimes comical, of a man grown old, who is taking stock of his whole life as it lies behind him.

Let us go then, you and I,
When the evening is spread out against the sky
Like a patient etherised upon a table;
Let us go, through certain half-deserted streets,
The muttering retreats
Of restless nights in one-night cheap hotels
And sawdust restaurants with oyster-shells:
Streets that follow like a tedious argument
Of insidious intent
To lead you to an overwhelming question . . .

Oh, do not ask, 'What is it?'
Let us go and make our visit.

In the room the women come and go
Talking of Michelangelo.

The yellow fog that rubs its back upon the window-panes,
The yellow smoke that rubs its muzzle on the window-
panes,
Licked its tongue into the corners of the evening,
Lingered upon the pools that stand in drains,
Let fall upon its back the soot that falls from chimneys,
Slipped by the terrace, made a sudden leap,
And seeing that it was a soft October night,
Curled once about the house, and fell asleep.

16 May • *from* Craving For Spring • D. H. Lawrence

D. H. Lawrence often writes with a sense of elemental urgency, and in this poem the speaker is impatient for spring to appear, eager to move beyond the pale, portentous first-flowers – the snowdrops and early crocuses – towards the season's full, surging vitality.

I wish it were spring in the world.

Let it be spring!
Come, bubbling, surging tide of sap!
Come, rush of creation!
Come, life! surge through this mass of mortification!
Come, sweep away these exquisite, ghastly first-flowers,
which are rather last-flowers!
Come, thaw down their cool portentousness, dissolve them:
snowdrops, straight, death-veined exhalations of white and
    purple crocuses,
flowers of the penumbra, issue of corruption, nourished in
    mortification,
jets of exquisite finality;
Come, spring, make havoc of them!

I trample on the snowdrops, it gives me pleasure to tread
    down the jonquils,
to destroy the chill Lent lilies;
for I am sick of them, their faint-bloodedness,
slow-blooded, icy-fleshed, portentous.

I want the fine, kindling wine-sap of spring,
gold, and of inconceivably fine, quintessential brightness,
rare almost as beams, yet overwhelmingly potent,
strong like the greatest force of world-balancing.

This is the same that picks up the harvest of wheat
and rocks it, tons of grain, on the ripening wind;
the same that dangles the globe-shaped pleiads of fruit
temptingly in mid-air, between a playful thumb and finger;
oh, and suddenly, from out of nowhere, whirls the pear-bloom,
upon us, and apple- and almond- and apricot- and quince-
    blossom,
storms and cumulus clouds of all imaginable blossom
about our bewildered faces,
though we do not worship.

I wish it were spring
cunningly blowing on the fallen sparks, odds and ends of the
    old, scattered fire,
and kindling shapely little conflagrations
curious long-legged foals, and wide-eared calves, and naked
    sparrow-bubs.

I wish that spring
would start the thundering traffic of feet
new feet on the earth, beating with impatience.

I wish it were spring, thundering
delicate, tender spring.
I wish these brittle, frost-lovely flowers of passionate,
    mysterious corruption
were not yet to come still more from the still-flickering
    discontent.

Oh, in the spring, the bluebell bows him down for very
exuberance,
exulting with secret warm excess,
bowed down with his inner magnificence!

Oh, yes, the gush of spring is strong enough
to toss the globe of earth like a ball on a water-jet
dancing sportfully;
as you see a tiny celluloid ball tossing on a squirt of water
for men to shoot at, penny-a-time, in a booth at a fair.

. . .

Ah come, come quickly, spring!
come and lift us towards our culmination, we myriads;
we who have never flowered, like patient cactuses.
Come and lift us to our end, to blossom, bring us to our
summer,
we who are winter-weary in the winter of the of the world.
Come making the chaffinch nests hollow and cosy,
come and soften the willow buds till they are puffed and furred,
then blow them over with gold.
Coma and cajole the gawky colt's-foot flowers.

16 May • Apple Blossom • Louis MacNeice

In this poem, Louis MacNeice reminds us that repeated experiences do not necessarily have to diminish the sense of wonderment that we once had as inquisitive children. Just as Adam and Eve lost their innocence and were exiled from Eden to find that the world outside was no less beautiful, the sky no less blue, then so too we, MacNeice suggests, have the ability to see things anew even now we're adults, cast out from the Eden of childhood.

The first blossom was the best blossom
For the child who never had seen an orchard;
For the youth whom whiskey had led astray
The morning after was the first day.

The first apple was the best apple
For Adam before he heard the sentence;
When the flaming sword endorsed the Fall
The trees were his to plant for all.

The first ocean was the best ocean
For the child from streets of doubt and litter;
For the youth for whom the skies unfurled
His first love was his first world.

But the first verdict seemed the worst verdict
When Adam and Eve were expelled from Eden,
Yet when the bitter gates clanged to
The sky beyond was just as blue.

For the next ocean is the first ocean
And the last ocean is the first ocean
And, however often the sun may rise,
A new thing dawns upon our eyes.

For the last blossom is the first blossom
And the first blossom is the last blossom
And when from Eden we take our way
The morning after is the first day.

17 May • A Handsome Young Fellow Called Frears • Michael Palin

Michael Palin is one of the men behind the British comedy outfit Monty Python. He is a master of the limerick form: first there is a pair of long rhyming lines, then a pair of short rhyming lines, and then a final line returns us to the rhyme of the opening lines. Limericks, named after the Irish county of Limerick, can be identified by their sound as much as their appearance on the page.

A handsome young fellow called Frears
Was attracted to girls by their ears.
He'd traverse the globe
For a really nice lobe,
And the sight would reduce him to tears.

17 May • Aunt Julia • Norman MacCaig

In this poem, the Scottish poet Norman MacCaig is writing about his aunt. His Aunt Julia worked as a crofter, which is a small-scale farmer. She only spoke Gaelic, a Celtic language native to Scotland, and MacCaig's poem is full of the regret he feels that he only learned the language after she had died.

Aunt Julia spoke Gaelic
very loud and very fast.
I could not answer her –
I could not understand her.

She wore men's boots
when she wore any.
— I can see her strong foot,
stained with peat,
paddling with the treadle of the spinningwheel
while her right hand drew yarn
marvellously out of the air.

Hers was the only house
where I've lain at night
in the absolute darkness
of a box bed, listening to
crickets being friendly.

She was buckets
and water flouncing into them.
She was winds pouring wetly
round house-ends.
She was brown eggs, black skirts
and a keeper of threepennybits
in a teapot.

Aunt Julia spoke Gaelic
very loud and very fast.
By the time I had learned
a little, she lay
silenced in the absolute black
of a sandy grave
at Luskentyre. But I hear her still, welcoming me
with a seagull's voice
across a hundred yards
of peatscrapes and lazybeds
and getting angry, getting angry
with so many questions
unanswered.

18 May • Matilda: Who Told Lies, and was Burned to Death • Hilaire Belloc

The poem is a cautionary verse, one that serves as a playful warning to its readers. It is in many respects a poetic retelling of one of Aesop's fables, 'The Boy Who Cried Wolf'.

Matilda told such Dreadful Lies,
It made one Gasp and Stretch one's Eyes;
Her Aunt, who, from her Earliest Youth,
Had kept a Strict Regard for Truth,
Attempted to Believe Matilda:
The effort very nearly killed her,
And would have done so, had not She
Discovered this Infirmity.
For once, towards the Close of Day,
Matilda, growing tired of play,
And finding she was left alone,
Went tiptoe to the Telephone
And summoned the Immediate Aid
Of London's Noble Fire-Brigade.
Within an hour the Gallant Band
Were pouring in on every hand,
From Putney, Hackney Downs, and Bow.
With Courage high and Hearts a-glow,
They galloped, roaring through the Town,
'Matilda's House is Burning Down!'
Inspired by British Cheers and Loud
Proceeding from the Frenzied Crowd,
They ran their ladders through a score
Of windows on the Ball Room Floor;

And took Peculiar Pains to Souse
The Pictures up and down the House,
Until Matilda's Aunt succeeded
In showing them they were not needed;
And even then she had to pay
To get the Men to go away!
It happened that a few Weeks later
Her Aunt was off to the Theatre
To see that Interesting Play
The Second Mrs Tanqueray.
She had refused to take her Niece
To hear this Entertaining Piece:
A Deprivation Just and Wise
To Punish her for Telling Lies.
That Night a Fire *did* break out –
You should have heard Matilda Shout!
You should have heard her Scream and Bawl,
And throw the window up and call
To People passing in the Street –
(The rapidly increasing Heat
Encouraging her to obtain
Their confidence) – but all in vain!
For every time She shouted 'Fire!'
They only answered 'Little Liar!'
And therefore when her Aunt returned,
Matilda, and the House, were Burned.

18 May • The Moment • Margaret Atwood

Although we often seem to link the idea of being 'at home' somewhere with owning it, this poem looks at the matter in a different way.

The moment when, after many years
of hard work and a long voyage
you stand in the centre of your room,
house, half-acre, square mile, island, country,
knowing at last how you got there,
and say, I own this,

is the same moment when the trees unloose
their soft arms from around you,
the birds take back their language,
the cliffs fissure and collapse,
the air moves back from you like a wave
and you can't breathe.

No, they whisper. You own nothing.
You were a visitor, time after time
climbing the hill, planting the flag, proclaiming.
We never belonged to you.
You never found us.
It was always the other way round.

19 May • Oranges and Lemons • Anon.

On 19 May 1536, Anne Boleyn was executed. She was the second wife of Henry VIII, and mother of the future Queen Elizabeth I. Anne was married to Henry for only three years before he began courting Jane Seymour, at which point he ended his marriage to Anne by putting her on trial for treason and having her beheaded. It is popularly believed that the nursery rhyme 'Oranges and Lemons', with its final lines, relates to execution by beheading, and that it may even be modelled on Henry VIII's relationships. The line 'Here comes a chopper to chop off your head' also appears at a crucial moment in George Orwell's *Nineteen Eighty-Four*. When read aloud, the poem is said to mimic the distinctive sounds of the bells it describes.

Oranges and lemons,
Say the bells of St Clement's.

You owe me five farthings,
Say the bells of St Martin's.

When will you pay me?
Say the bells of Old Bailey.

When I grow rich,
Say the bells of Shoreditch.

When will that be?
Say the bells of Stepney.

I'm sure I don't know,
Says the great bell of Bow.

Here comes a candle to light you to bed,
Here comes a chopper to chop off your head.
Chip chop, chip chop, the last man is dead.

19 May • One Art • Elizabeth Bishop

At the beginning of this poem, Elizabeth Bishop half-jokingly suggests that you should practise 'the art of losing' by losing small, material things like house keys and watches, so you're prepared for the larger, more difficult losses to come.

The art of losing isn't hard to master;
so many things seem filled with the intent
to be lost that their loss is no disaster.

Lose something every day. Accept the fluster
of lost door keys, the hour badly spent.
The art of losing isn't hard to master.

Then practise losing farther, losing faster:
places, and names, and where it was you meant
to travel. None of these will bring disaster.

I lost my mother's watch. And look! my last, or
next-to-last, of three loved houses went.
The art of losing isn't hard to master.

I lost two cities, lovely ones. And, vaster,
some realms I owned, two rivers, a continent.
I miss them, but it wasn't a disaster.

—Even losing you (the joking voice, a gesture
I love) I shan't have lied. It's evident
the art of losing's not too hard to master
though it may look like (Write it!) like disaster.

20 May • Courage • Amelia Earhart

On 20 May 1932, Amelia Earhart made history as the first female to complete a transatlantic flight. Departing from Harbour Grace, Newfoundland, in the morning, Earhart flew for 14 hours and 56 minutes before landing just north of Derry in Northern Ireland. Famed for her daring and ambition, it is perhaps no surprise that this poem by Earhart takes courage as its topic.

Courage is the price that Life exacts for granting peace.

The soul that knows it not knows no release
From little things:

Knows not the livid loneliness of fear,
Nor mountain heights where bitter joy can hear
The sound of wings.

How can life grant us boon of living, compensate
For dull gray ugliness and pregnant hate
Unless we dare

The soul's dominion? Each time we make a choice, we pay
With courage to behold the resistless day,
And count it fair.

'The Mouse's Tale' from *Alice's Adventures in Wonderland* is a great picture poem – a verse form that is shaped like its subject matter. Appearing early on in the novel, a mouse begins to tell Alice a sad story, its 'tale'. All Alice can focus on is its real tail, and the two soon are woven together in a classic nonsense poem.

'Fury said to
a mouse, That
he met in the
house, "Let
us both go
to law: *I*
will prose-
cute you.—
Come, I'll
take no de-
nial; We
must have
the trial:
For really
this morn-
ing I've
nothing
to do."
Said the
mouse to
the cur,
"Such a
trial, dear
Sir, With
no jury
or judge,
would
be wast-
ing our
breath."
"I'll be
judge,
I'll be
jury,"
Said
cun-
ning
old
Fury;
"I'll
try
the
whole
cause,
and
condemn
you to
death."'

21 May • Friends • Polly Clark

Poems take their source material from many places. Some focus on the poet's own experiences, others draw from previous literary works and, in this case, the poem is inspired by the American sitcom *Friends*.

It showed how friendship
doesn't end (like when
Emma and I watched

eight episodes in one go)
though outside my window
the climate was changing

and in my experience
people found each other
quite easy to take or leave.

The day after the last episode
they ran them all again,
protecting me, it seems.

I keep just one from
Two-hundred-and-thirty-six.
It's the one where Ross says,

but this can't be it,
and Rachel says,
then how come it is?

and he sinks to his knees with his arms
around her legs and the camera
moves slowly back

and they hold the shot
for a long time
before the theme tune begins.

21 May • Little Orphant Annie • James Whitcomb Riley

This poem, which was first published in 1885, is based in part on an orphan who lived with the poet's family, and told stories about children being snatched away by goblins and elves if they ever misbehaved. It is written in Hoosier dialect which originates from Indiana in America.

Little Orphant Annie's come to our house to stay,
An' wash the cups an' saucers up, an' brush the crumbs away,
An' shoo the chickens off the porch, an' dust the hearth, an'
    sweep,
An' make the fire, an' bake the bread, an' earn her board-
    an'-keep;
An' all us other childern, when the supper things is done,
We set around the kitchen fire an' has the mostest fun
A-list'nin' to the witch-tales 'at Annie tells about,
An' the Gobble-uns 'at gits you
        Ef you
          Don't
            Watch
              Out!

Onc't they was a little boy wouldn't say his prayers,–
So when he went to bed at night, away up stairs,
His Mammy heerd him holler, an' his Daddy heerd him bawl,
An' when they turn't the kivvers down, he wasn't there at all!
An' they seeked him in the rafter-room, an' cubby-hole, an'
press,
An' seeked him up the chimbly-flue, an' ever'wheres, I guess;
But all they ever found was thist his pants an' roundabout–
An' the Gobble-uns'll git you
Ef you
Don't
Watch
Out!

An' one time a little girl 'ud allus laugh an' grin,
An' make fun of ever'one, an' all her blood an' kin;
An' onc't, when they was 'company', an' ole folks was there,
She mocked 'em an' shocked 'em, an' said she didn't care!
An' thist as she kicked her heels, an' turn't to run an' hide,
They was two great big Black Things a-standin' by her side,
An' they snatched her through the ceilin' 'fore she knowed
what she's about!
An' the Gobble-uns'll git you
Ef you
Don't
Watch
Out!

An' little Orphant Annie says when the blaze is blue,
An' the lamp-wick sputters, an' the wind goes woo-oo!
An' you hear the crickets quit, an' the moon is gray,
An' the lightnin'-bugs in dew is all squenched away,–
You better mind yer parents, an' yer teachers fond an' dear,
An' churish them 'at loves you, an' dry the orphant's tear,
An' he'p the pore an' needy ones 'at clusters all about,
Er the Gobble-uns'll git you
Ef you
Don't
Watch
Out!

22 May • Today Is Very Boring • Jack Prelutsky

Boredom is a state of mind – sometimes if you decide you are bored, then you might miss the truly exciting stuff in life. That is Jack Prelutsky's message, and he pushes it to some extreme examples.

Today is very boring,
it's a very boring day,
there is nothing much to look at,
there is nothing much to say,
there's a peacock on my sneakers,
there's a penguin on my head,
there's a dormouse on my doorstep,
I am going back to bed.

Today is very boring,
it is boring through and through,
there is absolutely nothing
that I think I want to do,
I see giants riding rhinos,
and an ogre with a sword,
there's a dragon blowing smoke rings,
I am positively bored.

Today is very boring,
I can hardly help but yawn,
there's a flying saucer landing
in the middle of my lawn,
a volcano just erupted
less than half a mile away,
and I think I felt an earthquake,
it's a very boring day.

22 May • Jim, Who Ran Away from his Nurse and Was Eaten by a Lion • Hilaire Belloc

A 'nurse' is a word that was used for the women who looked after small children, just as nannies and childminders do nowadays. In this poem, Hilaire Belloc tells the cautionary tale of Jim, who ran away from his nurse. Although the subject of the poem is dark, the rhyming couplets and the humorous tone make it comic.

There was a Boy whose name was Jim;
His Friends were very good to him.
They gave him Tea, and Cakes, and Jam,
And slices of delicious Ham,
And Chocolate with pink inside
And little Tricycles to ride,
And read him Stories through and through,
And even took him to the Zoo—
But there it was the dreadful Fate
Befell him, which I now relate.

You know—or at least you ought to know,
For I have often told you so—
That Children never are allowed
To leave their Nurses in a Crowd;
Now this was Jim's especial Foible,
He ran away when he was able,
And on this inauspicious day
He slipped his hand and ran away!

He hadn't gone a yard when—Bang!
With open Jaws, a lion sprang,
And hungrily began to eat
The Boy: beginning at his feet.
Now, just imagine how it feels
When first your toes and then your heels,
And then by gradual degrees,
Your shins and ankles, calves and knees,
Are slowly eaten, bit by bit.
No wonder Jim detested it!
No wonder that he shouted 'Hi!'

The Honest Keeper heard his cry,
Though very fat he almost ran
To help the little gentleman.
'Ponto!' he ordered as he came
(For Ponto was the Lion's name),
'Ponto!' he cried, with angry Frown,
'Let go, Sir! Down, Sir! Put it down!'
The Lion made a sudden stop,
He let the Dainty Morsel drop,
And slunk reluctant to his Cage,
Snarling with Disappointed Rage.
But when he bent him over Jim,
The Honest Keeper's Eyes were dim.
The Lion having reached his Head,
The Miserable Boy was dead!

When Nurse informed his Parents, they
Were more Concerned than I can say:—
His Mother, as She dried her eyes,
Said, 'Well—it gives me no surprise,
He would not do as he was told!'
His Father, who was self-controlled,
Bade all the children round attend
To James's miserable end,
And always keep a-hold of Nurse
For fear of finding something worse.

23 May • A Tragic Story • William Makepeace Thackeray

William Makepeace Thackeray's poem gives a serious name and a sombre tone to what is actually a silly subject: a man trying to escape his own pigtail.

There lived a sage in days of yore,
And he a handsome pigtail wore:
But wondered much, and sorrowed more,
  Because it hung behind him.

He mused upon this curious case,
And swore he'd change the pigtail's place,
And have it hanging at his face,
  Not dangling there behind him.

Says he, 'The mystery I've found –
Says he, 'The mystery I've found!
I'll turn me round,' – he turned him round;
  But still it hung behind him.

Then round and round, and out and in,
All day the puzzled sage did spin;
In vain – it mattered not a pin –
  The pigtail hung behind him.

And right and left and round about,
And up and down, and in and out
He turned; but still the pigtail stout
  Hung steadily behind him.

And though his efforts never slack,
And though he twist, and twirl, and tack,
Alas! still faithful to his back,
  The pigtail hangs behind him.

23 May • Bookworm • Anon., translated by Michael Alexander

When we use the term 'bookworm', we generally mean a person who loves to read. Here, however, an anonymous medieval poet is playing on the double meaning of the term: a bookworm can also be an actual worm, or maggot, that feeds on paper.

A worm ate words. I thought that wonderfully
Strange – a miracle – when they told me a crawling
Insect had swallowed noble songs,
A night-time thief had stolen writing
So famous, so weighty. But the bug was foolish
Still, though its belly was full of thought.

24 May • Buddha • Tony Mitton

Vesak, or Buddha Day, is celebrated on the full moon of the Indian lunar month of Vesakha, which is usually in May. It is one of the most important festivals in the Buddhist calendar as it commemorates three significant events in Gautama Buddha's life – his birth, his enlightenment and his death.

The Buddha is not a god,
but human.

The Buddha's image
is not an icon to be worshipped.

The Buddha is you,
is me.

The Buddha you see
is just a reminder.

It says, simply,
'All you need is this,
this quiet sitting.
The answer is inside you.
You carry it like a seed.

Only listen inwardly
to stillness and to silence,
beneath all thought,
emotion and sensation,

to know the lotus
as its flower unfolds.'

24 May • A Riddle • Christina Rossetti

Can you guess the answer to this riddle by Christina Rossetti? (Answer underneath!)

There is one that has a head without an eye,
  And there is one that has an eye without a head.
You may find the answer if you try;
  And when all is said,
  Half the answer hangs upon a thread.

The answer to this riddle is 'a pin and a needle'.

25 May • The Riddle Song • Anon.

'The Riddle Song' contains four riddles in one poem. In the final verse, the poem surprisingly supplies all the answers to its own questions.

My love gave me a chicken, but it had no bone.
My love gave me a cherry, but it had no stone.
My love gave me a scare, without a single shiver.
My love showed me a bridge without a running river.

How can there be a chicken, without a bone?
How can there be a cherry, without a stone?
How can there be a scare, without a single shiver?
How can there be a bridge, without a running river?

When the chicken is in the egg, there is no bone.
When the cherry is in the blossom, there is no stone.
When the scare is in the field, to frighten off the crows.
When the bridge is on the face and runs across the nose.

25 May • *from* The Ballad of Reading Gaol • Oscar Wilde

Wilde wrote these lines, a reflection on his two-year imprisonment, from exile in France. He was incarcerated because of his sexuality, and he endured abominable treatment as an inmate. In this extract, Wilde compares treatment in prison with the very crimes committed by prisoners.

I know not whether Laws be right,
 Or whether Laws be wrong;
All that we know who lie in gaol
 Is that the wall is strong;
And that each day is like a year,
 A year whose days are long.

But this I know, that every Law
 That men have made for Man,
Since first Man took his brother's life,
 And the sad world began,
But straws the wheat and saves the chaff
 With a most evil fan.

This too I know – and wise it were
 If each could know the same –
That every prison that men build
 Is built with bricks of shame,
And bound with bars lest Christ should see
 How men their brothers maim.

With bars they blur the gracious moon,
And blind the goodly sun;
And they do well to hide their Hell,
For in it things are done
That Son of God nor son of Man
Ever should look upon!

26 May • Full Moon • Vita Sackville-West

Vita Sackville-West was part of the illustrious Bloomsbury Group – a collective of writers, artists and intellectuals in the early twentieth century that included Virginia Woolf, E. M. Forster and the economist John Maynard Keynes. There is a sense of both gaiety and mystery in this poem.

She was wearing coral taffeta trousers
Someone had brought her from Isfahan,
And the little gold coat with pomegranate blossoms,
And the coral-hafted feather fan,
But she ran down a Kentish lane in the moonlight,
And skipped in the pool of moon as she ran.

She cared not a rap for all the big planets,
For Betelgeuse or Aldebaran,
And all the big planets cared nothing for her,
That small impertinent charlatan,
But she climbed on a Kentish stile in the moonlight,
And laughed at the sky through the sticks of her fan.

26 May • One Fine Day in the Middle of the Night • Anon.

This poem is a nonsense rhyme; even the title makes no sense. You're right not to believe a word of it. The poet is playing a game: how many impossible things can fit into a short rhyming poem?

One fine day in the middle of the night,
Two dead boys got up to fight,
Back to back they faced each other,
Drew their swords and shot each other,
One was blind and the other couldn't see
So they chose a dummy for a referee.
A blind man went to see fair play,
A dumb man went to shout 'hooray!'
A paralysed donkey passing by,
Kicked the blind man in the eye,
Knocked him through a nine inch wall,
Into a dry ditch and drowned them all,
A deaf policeman heard the noise,
And came to arrest the two dead boys.
If you don't believe this story's true,
Ask the blind man he saw it too!

27 May • God's Grandeur • Gerard Manley Hopkins

Whitsun, or Whit Sunday, falls on the seventh Sunday after Easter. It commemorates the Holy Spirit's descent upon the disciples of Jesus. In the north of England, there are parades known as 'Whit Walks' on and around Whitsun. Hopkins's extraordinary lines describe the 'Holy Ghost' as it hangs above the world, and they form a tight and knotty poem that should be read aloud for full effect.

The world is charged with the grandeur of God.
  It will flame out, like shining from shook foil;
  It gathers to a greatness, like the ooze of oil
Crushed. Why do men then now not reck his rod?
Generations have trod, have trod, have trod;
  And all is seared with trade; bleared, smeared with toil;
  And wears man's smudge and shares man's smell: the soil
Is bare now, nor can foot feel, being shod.

And for all this, nature is never spent;
  There lives the dearest freshness deep down things;
And though the last lights off the black West went
  Oh, morning, at the brown brink eastward, springs –
Because the Holy Ghost over the bent
  World broods with warm breast and with ah! bright wings.

27 May • M.O.R.E.R.A.P.S • Joseph Coelho

When we discuss poetry, we often use many complex words, such as 'onomatopoeia', 'metaphor' and 'alliteration'. This poem by former children's laureate Joseph Coelho is particularly useful for helping children to remember all the different definitions.

The M.O.R.E.R.A.P.S are a trick
to help with your writing.
They add a kick to language,
Make writing more exciting.

M is for Metaphor –
saying one thing is another.
'The sun is an oven.'
'The Earth is everyone's mother.'

O is for Onomatopoeia –
words that are also sounds.
'Whoosh went the wind.'
'Howl went the hound.'

R is for Rhyme –
words that sound the same.
You can put a cat in a hat.
Or simply try rhyming your name.

E is for Emotion –
happy, worried and sad.
Great writing shares a feeling
from the good to the bad.

R is for Repetition –
But don't repeat any old word!
Find a phrase with a musical rhythm
that sounds like a song from a bird.

A is for Alliteration –
words sharing the same starting letter,
used in the tongue-twister
that made Betty's bitter batter better.

P is for Personification –
human features ascribed to a thing.
I looked to the sky and saw
the sun's bright shining grin.

S is for Simile –
using 'as' and 'like' to compare.
For instance, 'When Mother gets angry
she snarls like a rampaging bear.'

The M.O.R.E.R.A.P.S are a wonderful way
to add a punch to your writing.
Master them like a juggler.
make your words ripe for the biting.

28 May • I Am! • John Clare

This poem, one of Clare's most popular, was written during his second period in an asylum. It is full of anguish and self-pity. However, the poem's opening words – 'I am' – are defiant, and no matter what has happened in the past, and no matter what Clare wishes for the future, one thing remains certain in his troubled mind: he still exists.

I am: yet what I am none cares or knows,
  My friends forsake me like a memory lost;
I am the self-consumer of my woes,
  They rise and vanish in oblivious host,
Like shades in love and death's oblivion lost;
And yet I am, and live with shadows tost

Into the nothingness of scorn and noise,
  Into the living sea of waking dreams,
Where there is neither sense of life nor joys,
  But the vast shipwreck of my life's esteems;
And e'en the dearest – that I loved the best –
Are strange – nay, rather stranger than the rest.

I long for scenes where man has never trod,
  A place where woman never smiled or wept;
There to abide with my Creator, God,
  And sleep as I in childhood sweetly slept:
Untroubling and untroubled where I lie,
The grass below – above the vaulted sky.

28 May • Yes • Adrian Mitchell

In this poem, different things speak to illustrate what they can mean to us. While some of the things 'spoken' in this poem are comic, like the kangaroo saying 'trampoline', others have deeper meanings, such as the soldier crying 'Mother'!

A smile says: Yes.
A heart says: Blood.
When the rain says: Drink.
The earth says: Mud.

The kangaroo says: Trampoline.
Giraffes say: Tree.
A bus says: Us.
While a car says: Me.

Lemon trees say: Lemons.
A jug says: Lemonade.
The villain says: You're wonderful.
The hero: I'm afraid.

The forest says: Hide and Seek.
The grass says: Green and Grow.
The railway says: Maybe.
The prison says: No.

The millionaire says: Take.
The beggar says: Give.
The soldier cries: Mother!
The baby sings: Live.

The river says: Come with me.
The moon says: Bless.
The stars say: Enjoy the light.
The sun says: Yes.

29 May • *from* Everest Climbed • Ian Serraillier

On this day in 1953, the New Zealander Edmund Hillary and the Nepalese Tenzing Norgay became the first confirmed climbers to have reached the summit of Mount Everest, the tallest mountain in the world. Everest sits on the border of Nepal and China, and its summit is 8,848 metres above sea level – for comparison, the highest point in England, Scafell Pike is 978 metres. The first full ascent of Everest remains one of the most remarkable moments in human exploration, comparable with reaching the North Pole or walking on the moon. And yet Hillary's notes from the summit are quite plain: 'We made seats for ourselves in the snow, and sitting there in reasonable comfort we ate with relish a bar of mint cake.'

And now with a sickening shock
They saw before them a towering wall
Of smooth and holdless rock.
O ghastly fear – with the goal so near
To find the way was blocked!
On one side darkly the mountain dropped,
On the other two plunging miles of peak
Shot from the dizzy skyline down
In a silver streak.

'No hope of turning the bluff to the west,'
Said Hillary. 'What's that I see to the east?
A worm-wide crack between cornice and rock –
Will it hold? I can try it at least.'

He called to Tenzing, 'Draw in the slack!'
Then levered himself right into the crack
And, kicking his spikes in the frozen crust,
Wriggled up with his back.
With arms and feet and shoulders he fought,
Inch by sweating inch, then caught
At the crest and grabbed for the light of day.
There was time, as he struggled for breath, to pray
For all the might that a man could wish –
Then he heaved at the rope till over the lip
Brave Tenzing, hauled from the deep, fell flop
Like a monstrous gaping fish.

Was the summit theirs? – they puffed and panted –
No, for the ridge still upward pointed.
On they plodded, Martian-weird
With pouting mask and icicle beard
That cracked and tinkled, broke and rattled,
As on with pound hearts they battled,
On to the summit –
Till at last the ridge began to drop.
Two swings, two whacks of Hillary's axe,
And they stoop at the top.

This tale of heroes is ended, the trumpets all
Have sounded. Soon, in the glass of history, we shall see
Their triumph – no boyish adventure, no trick of vanity
fulfilled,
But a march in man's long progress to the stars.
And their glory shines in being, not in doing –
In courage, humanity, and valour uncomplaining.
It is the tale of Man himself, who made
The sea his highroad and the lonely sky his wing-way,
Who defied the world's highest stronghold and won
Her crown of snow.

29 May • There was a Young Lady whose Chin • Edward Lear

This limerick by Edward Lear creates the comical picture of the Young Lady of the title playing the harp using only her exceedingly pointy chin.

There was a Young Lady whose chin
Resembled the point of a pin;
So she had it made sharp,
And purchased a harp,
And played several tunes with her chin.

30 May • Life Doesn't Frighten Me • Maya Angelou

Because she lived such a full life herself, Angelou sets an authoritative example when she writes that life is nothing to fear. But it is a young child in this poem who is so defiant and fearless.

Shadows on the wall
Noises down the hall
Life doesn't frighten me at all
Bad dogs barking loud
Big ghosts in a cloud
Life doesn't frighten me at all.

Mean old Mother Goose
Lions on the loose
They don't frighten me at all
Dragons breathing flame
On my counterpane
That doesn't frighten me at all.

I go boo
Make them shoo
I make fun
Way they run
I won't cry
So they fly
I just smile
They go wild
Life doesn't frighten me at all.

Tough guys fight
All alone at night
Life doesn't frighten me at all
Panthers in the park
Strangers in the dark
No, they don't frighten me at all.

That new classroom where
Boys all pull my hair
(Kissy little girls
With their hair in curls)
They don't frighten me at all.

Don't show me frogs and snakes
And listen for my scream,
If I'm afraid at all
It's only in my dreams.

I've got a magic charm
That I keep up my sleeve,
I can walk the ocean floor
And never have to breathe.

Life doesn't frighten me at all
Not at all
Not at all.
Life doesn't frighten me at all.

30 May • Joan of Arc • Florence Earle Coates

On 30 May 1431, the French military leader Joan of Arc, a famous figure in the Hundred Years War between France and England, was burnt at the stake. It is thought that she was only nineteen years old at the time. This poem by Florence Earle Coates was written in 1916, and praises Joan's extraordinary life.

Her spirit is to France a living spring
  From which to draw deep draughts of life. To-day,—
  As when a peasant girl she led the way
Victorious to Rheims and crowned the King,—
High and heroic thoughts about her cling,
  And sacrificial faiths as pure as they,
  Moving the land she loved, with gentle sway,
To be, for love of her, a better thing!
Was she unhappy? No: her radiant youth
  Burned, like a meteor, on to swift eclipse;
  But where it passed, there lingers still a light.
She waited, wistful, for the word of truth
  That breathed in blessing from immortal lips
  When earthly comfort failed, and all around was night.

31 May • The Man He Killed • Thomas Hardy

The second Boer War, which started in 1899, ended on this day in 1902. It was a bloody war, fought in what is now South Africa between the British and the Boer armies. Around the world, opposition to the war was strong, and there were many British citizens who objected to it. Hardy's poem, published during the war, reflects on the absurdity and mindlessness of armed conflict.

'Had he and I but met
By some old ancient inn,
We should have sat us down to wet
Right many a nipperkin!

'But ranged as infantry,
And staring face to face,
I shot at him as he at me,
And killed him in his place.

'I shot him dead because –
Because he was my foe,
Just so: my foe of course he was:
That's clear enough; although

'He thought he'd 'list, perhaps,
Off-hand like – just as I –
Was out of work – had sold his traps –
No other reason why.

'Yes; quaint and curious war is!
You shoot a fellow down
You'd treat if met where any bar is,
Or help to half-a-crown.'

31 May • This is Just to Say • William Carlos Williams

We end the book with this wonderfully playful poem by the twentieth-century American Imagist poet William Carlos Williams. Although the poem has the single image of the missing plums in the icebox, it raises countless questions about who the icebox thief is, and what their relationship is with the poor fruit owner. The poem's last lines leave us with a fittingly refreshing feeling for the summer days just ahead.

I have eaten
the plums
that were in
the icebox

and which
you were probably
saving
for breakfast

Forgive me
they were delicious
so sweet
and so cold

Index of First Lines

Index of Poets and Translators

Acknowledgements

The compiler and publisher would like to thank the following for permission to use copyright material:

Agard, John: 'What the teacher said when asked: What er we vain for geography, Miss?' and 'A Date with Spring', copyright © John Agard 1983. Reproduced by kind permission of John Agard c/o Caroline Sheldon Literary Agency Ltd.; **Al-Massri, Maram:** 'Knocks on the Door' from *A Red Cherry on a White-tiled Floor*, trans. Khaled Mattawa (Bloodaxe Books, 2004). Reproduced with permission of Bloodaxe Books; **Angelou, Maya:** 'Life doesn't frighten me' and 'Phenomenal Woman' from *The Complete Poetry,* copyright © Maya Angelou 2015. Reprinted by permission of Virago, an imprint of Little, Brown Book Group; **Atwood, Margaret:** 'The Moment', reproduced with permission of Curtis Brown Group Ltd., London on behalf of Margaret Atwood, *Morning in the Burned House*, copyright © Margaret Atwood 1995; **Belloc, Hilaire:** 'Matilda: Who Told Lies, and was Burned to Death' from *Cautionary Verses* by Hilaire Belloc (Red Fox, 1995), copyright © Hilaire Belloc. Reprinted by permission of Peters Fraser + Dunlop Ltd. (www.petersfraserdunlop.com), 'Tarantella' from *Sonnets and Verse* by Hilaire Belloc, reprinted by permission of Peters Fraser + Dunlop (www.petersfraserdunlop.com) on behalf of the Estate of Hilaire Belloc, 'Jim, Who Ran Away from his Nurse and Was Eaten by a Lion' from *Cautionary Tales for Children* by Hilaire Belloc, reprinted by permission of Peters Fraser + Dunlop (www.petersfraserdunlop.com) on behalf of the Estate of Hilaire Belloc; **Berry, Wendell:** 'Anger Against Beasts' from *New Collected Poems*, copyright © Wendell Berry 2012. Reprinted by permission of Counterpoint Press; **Bishop, Elizabeth:** 'One Art' from *Poems: The Centenary Edition* by Elizabeth Bishop (Chatto & Windus, 2011) by permission of Penguin Random House; **Brownlee, Liz:** 'The Battle of the Sexes', by permission of the author; **Calder, Dave:** 'Silkie', by permission of the author; **Carter, James:** 'Love You More' by James Carter, reproduced with permission by Otter-Barry Books Ltd.; **Causley, Charles:** 'Ballad of the Bread Man', copyright © Charles Causley, from *Collected Poems for Children* (Macmillan Children's Books, 2016), used with permission of David Higham Associates on behalf of the estate of the author; **Clark, Polly:** 'Friends' from *Farewell My Lovely* (Bloodaxe Books, 2009). Reproduced with permission of Bloodaxe Books; **Clarke, John Cooper:** 'You Ain't Nothing but a Hedgehog', copyright © John Cooper Clarke, from *The Luckiest Guy Alive* (Picador, 2018). Used with permission Picador, London; **Coelho, Joseph:** 'M.O.R.E.R.A.P.S' from *Werewolf Club Rules*, written by Joseph Coelho, published by Frances Lincoln

Children's Books, an imprint of The Quarto Group, copyright © 2014. Reproduced by permission of Quarto Publishing Plc; **Collins, Billy:** 'Today' from *Nine Horses* (Picador, 2003) and 'The Lanyard' from *The Trouble with Poetry and other poems* (Picador, 2006), copyright © Billy Collins. Published by permission of Picador, London; **Cope, Wendy:** 'Waste Land Limericks' from *Two Cures for Love* (Faber & Faber Ltd., 2009), copyright © Wendy Cope 2016. Printed by permission of Faber & Faber Ltd.; **Cummings, E. E.:** 'o by the by', copyright © 1944, 1972, 1991 by the Trustees for the E. E. Cummings Trust, from *Completed Poems: 1904–1962* by E. E. Cummings, edited by George J. Firmage and 'in Just-' copyright © 1923, 1951, 1991 by the Trustees of E. E. Cummings Trust. Copyright © 1976 by George James Firmage; **de la Mare, Walter:** 'Tartary', copyright © Walter de la Mare. Reprinted by permission of The Literary Trustees of Walter de la Mare and The Society of Authors as their representative; **Dean, Jan:** 'Three Good Things', by permission of the author; **Duffy, Carol Ann:** 'Prior Knowledge' and 'Mrs Darwin' from *New and Collected Poems for Children* by Carol Ann Duffy. Published by Faber & Faber Ltd., 2017. Copyright © Carol Ann Duffy. Reproduced by permission of the author c/o Rogers, Coleridge & White Ltd., 20 Powis Mews, London W11 1JN; **Eliot, T. S.:** extract from 'The Wasteland' from *Wasteland and Other Poems* (Faber & Faber Ltd., 2002) copyright Set Copyrights Limited, 2015. All reproduced by permission of Faber & Faber Ltd.; **Farjeon, Eleanor:** 'A Morning Song' from *Blackbird Has Spoken* by Eleanor Farjeon (Macmillan Children's Books, 2000), copyright © Eleanor Farjeon; **Foster, John:** 'Spring Snow' from *The Poetry Chest* (Oxford University Press), copyright © John Foster 2007, included by permission of the author; **Gittins, Chrissie:** 'Holi', by permission of the author; **Glück, Louise:** 'Nostos' from *Meadowlands* by Louise Glück (Carcanet Press Limited, 1998), published by permission of Carcanet Press Limited; **Hill, Geoffrey:** 'Ode on the Loss of the *Titanic*' from *Selected Poems* (Penguin, 2006), copyright © Geoffrey Hill, 2006. Reprinted by permission of Penguin Random House; **Hoberman, Mary Ann:** 'Mayfly', copyright © 1976 by Mary Ann Hoberman, 'Brother', copyright © 1959 by Mary Ann Hoberman. Reprinted by permission of The Gina Maccoby Literary Agency; **Hollander, John:** 'Swan and Shadow' from *Types of Shape,* originally published by Yale University Press. Copyright © 1967, 1968, 1969, 1991 by John Hollander. Reproduced with permission of the Licensor through PLSclear; **Hughes, Ted:** 'The River in March' from *Season Songs* by Ted Hughes (Faber & Faber Ltd., 1985), copyright © The Estate of Ted Hughes, 2003, 'A Donkey' from *Collected Poems for Children* by Ted Hughes (Faber and Faber Ltd.). Published by permission of Faber and Faber Ltd.; **Johnson, Linton Kwesi:** 'Seasons of the Heart' from *Give the Ball to the Poet* (Commonwealth Education Trust, 2014); **Jones, Evan:** 'The Song of the Banana Man', by permission of Sadie Jones on behalf of the author; **Joseph, Jenny:** 'Warning', by permission of Johnson & Alcock Ltd.; **Komunyakaa, Yusef:** 'Facing It' from *Pleasure Dome* (Wesleyan University Press, 2014), copyright © Yusef Komunyakaa. Used with permission of the publisher; **Larkin, Philip:** 'The Trees' from *The Complete*

Poems (Faber & Faber Ltd., 2014), copyright © Philip Larkin. Printed by permission of Faber & Faber Ltd.; **MacCaig, Norman:** 'Toad' and 'Aunt Julia' from *The Poems of Norman MacCaig,* reproduced by permission of Polygon, an imprint of Birlinn Ltd. (www.birlinn.co.uk); **MacNeice, Louis:** 'April Fool' and 'Apple Blossom' from *Collected Poems* (Faber & Faber, 2016), copyright © Louise MacNeice. Published by permission of David Higham associates on behalf of the estate of the author; **McGough, Roger:** 'The Sound Collector' from *You Tell Me*, Viking Kestrel, by permission of Peters Fraser + Dunlop on behalf of the author; **McMillan, Ian:** 'Robinson Crusoe's Wise Sayings', by permission of the author; **Millay, Edna St Vincent:** 'The Fawn' copyright © Edna St Vincent Millay. Reproduced by permission of A. M. Heath & Co Ltd.; **Milne, A. A.:** 'Buckingham Palace', an extract from *When We Were Very Young* by A. A. Milne. 'The Emperor's Rhyme' from *Now We Are Six* by A. A. Milne. Text copyright © The Trustees of the Pooh Properties 1927. Published by Egmont UK Ltd. and used with permission; **Mitchell, Adrian:** 'Back in the Playground Blues', 'Song in Space' and 'Yes', copyright © Adrian Mitchell. Reproduced by permission of United Agents on behalf of The Estate of Adrian Mitchell; **Mitton, Tony:** 'Buddha', copyright © Tony Mitton 2020. This poem was first published in *Come Into This Poem* (Frances Lincoln, 2011). 'Awakening' and 'The Selkie Bride', copyright © Tony Mitton 2020. These poems were first published in *Plum* (Scholastic, 1998) and is currently published by Frances Lincoln (2010). These poems have been reproduced with permission from David Higham Associates UK; **Moses, Brian:** 'Dear Yuri' from *Lost Magic: The Very Best of Brian Moses,* copyright © Brian Moses 2016; **Palin, Michael:** 'A Handsome Young Fellow Called Frears' from *A Sackful of Limericks* (Random House Books, 2016), copyright © Michael Palin. Reprinted by permission of Penguin Random House; **Perera, Duranka:** 'Bitter State', with permission of the author; **Pound, Ezra:** 'In A Station of the Metro' from *Personae* by Ezra Pound (Faber and Faber Ltd.), published by permission of Faber and Faber Ltd.; **Prelutsky, Jack:** 'Today Is Very Boring' from *The New Kid on the Block* (Greenwillow Books, 1984), copyright © Jack Prelutsky, 1984; **Rieu, E. V.:** The Hippopotamus's Birthday', by permission of D. C. H. Rieu, Executor of the Estate of the author; **Robertson, Shauna Darling:** 'Dancing with Life', copyright © Shauna Darling Robertson. Printed with permission of the author; **Rooney, Rachel:** 'First Word' (After Helen Keller)', copyright © Rachel Rooney. Printed by permission of the author; **Sackville-West, Vita:** 'Full Moon', copyright © Vita Sackville-West. Reproduced with permission of Curtis Brown Group Ltd., London, on behalf of The Estate of Vita Sackville-West; **Seth, Vikram:** 'The Frog and the Nightingale' by Vikram Seth, copyright © Vikram Seth; **Smith, Stevie:** 'Human Affection' from *Collected Poems and Drawings* by Stevie Smith (Faber & Faber Ltd.), published by permission of Faber & Faber Ltd.; **Stevens, Roger:** 'Why the Bat Flies at Night', by permission of the author; **Tempest, Kae:** 'For my Niece' from *Hold Your Own,* copyright © Kae Tempest (Picador, 2014). Printed by permission of Picador; **Thomas, Dylan:** 'Evening hymn of the Reverend Eli

Jenkins' excerpt from *Under Milk Wood*, copyright © The Dylan Thomas Trust (Phoenix, 2014). Used with permission of David Higham Associates on behalf of the estate of the author; **Thomas, R. S:** 'The Bright Field' and 'Cynddylan on a Tractor' from *Collected Poems 1945–1990* (Orion, 2001), copyright © R. S. Thomas. Printed by permission of The Orion Publishing Group, London; **Williams, William Carlos:** 'This is Just to Say' from *Collected Poems Vol. 1 1909–1939* by William Carlos Williams (Carcanet Press Limited), published by permission of Carcanet Press Limited.

Every effort has been made to trace the copyright holders, but if any have been inadvertently overlooked the publisher will be pleased to make the necessary arrangement at the first opportunity.